MARKUS+DIANA

MARKUS + DIANA

Klaus Hagerup

TRANSLATED BY Tara Chace

FRONT STREET
Asheville, North Carolina

Originally published in Norway by H. Aschehoug & Co.
under the title *Markus og Diana*
Copyright © 1997 by Klaus Hagerup and H. Aschehoug & Co.
Printed in China
Designed by Helen Robinson
First U.S. edition

This translation has been published with the financial support of NORLA.

LIBRARY OF CONGRESS CATALOGING-IN-PUBLICATION DATA
Hagerup, Klaus.
[Aschehoug. English]
Markus and Diana / Klaus Hagerup.—1st U.S. ed.
p. cm.
Translated by Tara Chace.
Summary: A moment of false bravado and some imaginative letters allow
shy, anxiety-ridden, thirteen-year-old Markus to connect with a Hollywood star,
but when she returns home to Norway she wants to meet the
thirty-six-year-old millionaire she believes him to be.
ISBN-13: 978-1-932425-59-8 (alk. paper)
[1. Self-esteem—Fiction. 2. Actors and actresses—Fiction.
3. Friendship—Fiction. 4. Imagination—Fiction.
5. Letter writing—Fiction. 6. Norway—Fiction.]
I. Chace, Tara. II. Title.
PZ7.H12425Mar 2006
[Fic]—dc22
2005025567

FRONT STREET
An Imprint of Boyds Mills Press, Inc.
A Highlights Company

815 Church Street
Honesdale, Pennsylvania 18431

MARKUS+DIANA

CHAPTER 1 No one was a bigger coward than Wormster. Markus Simonsen who was afraid of heights and scared of the dark. Markus Simonsen who was sure lightning would strike him if he stepped on a crack in the sidewalk and who wouldn't dare take an elevator, even if it would save his life. Markus Simonsen who was afraid of spiders and dogs and just about everything else you could be afraid of in this world. Especially girls. They scared the hell out of him and all they had to do to make him blush was look at him. And they did that a lot. Even though he wasn't much to look at. Markus was the shortest, scrawniest boy in class 6B at Ruud Elementary School. He had sand-colored hair and thick glasses with brown frames. They made him look almost like an old man even though he was only thirteen. Actually, it wasn't just the glasses that made him look older than he was. It was also all the anxiety he carried around with him. When he walked back and forth across the playground with Sigmund, he moved slowly and kept his head bowed. "Like an old gnome," Reidar said. Reidar who had run 60 meters in 8.3 seconds and who had a mountain bike worth almost a thousand dollars. Markus didn't have a bike. The very idea of lurching along on a piece of scaffolding on wheels made him feel sick to his stomach. He'd rather walk to school. That could be perilous enough, he thought. Stray dogs and colorblind drivers who couldn't tell the difference between red and green.

You never knew. Better to be on the safe side. But was there really a side that was safe? Markus doubted it. He went through life as though he were walking a fine line.

The only person he hung out with, strangely enough, was Sigmund, the tallest, most talented boy in the class. Sigmund's father was a mathematician, and Sigmund had impressed the whole class with his essay about the origin of the universe. He wrote so matter-of-factly about the Big Bang, Black Holes, and the Universe, which was bending, that he might as well have been describing his summer vacation in the Canary Islands. And he had another skill that was unusual for a Norwegian sixth grader: He could read books written in English. No less than four of the girls in their class were secretly in love with Sigmund, something that didn't faze him at all.

"Look, Mona's staring at you," Markus whispered one day while they were strolling—because Sigmund and Markus didn't walk, they strolled—back and forth across the playground during recess.

"No," Sigmund said slowly, "she's staring at you."

Then Markus blushed and bent his head down even further.

"That's what I was afraid of," he whispered.

"If a girl stares at you, just stare back," Sigmund said. "That makes them stop staring right away."

"That's easy for you to say. You're five foot seven. I'm only four foot eleven and a half."

"Yeah," Sigmund said seriously, "I may not stop growing until I'm over ten feet tall."

"Then you'll be in the *Guinness Book of World Records*," Markus said.

"I don't want to be in the *Guinness Book of World Records*. I want to be an astrophysicist."

Markus didn't know what an astrophysicist was, but he didn't see why being one would keep you from getting into the *Guinness Book of World Records*, and he said so.

"How many astrophysicists do you think there are in the *Guinness Book of World Records*?" Sigmund asked.

"I don't know."

"Not a single one."

"Then you'll be the first one."

"If I'm ten feet tall, I won't have time to be an astrophysicist. There'll be too much commotion." Then Sigmund yelled, "Hi, Mona!"

Mona looked over at them. She noticed Sigmund looking at her and blushed.

"Have a lot to do, Mona?"

"Huh?"

"Are you done studying for the history test?"

"I … I don't know. What do you mean?"

"Well, if you're not done studying, I don't think you should be spending so much time staring at Wormster like that."

Mona blushed even more, opened the book she was holding in her hand, and pretended to concentrate on reading it.

"That's how you handle girls who are being too pushy," Sigmund said.

"Not me. That's how *you* handle them. Do you have to call me Wormster?"

"But everyone calls you Wormster."

"Yeah, but you could call me Markus."

"I'm your friend, aren't I?"

"Yeah."

"Well, that's why I call you Wormster," Sigmund said somberly. "Other people are going to do it anyway. If I do it too then it won't be an insult anymore. Then you'll get used to it."

"I will not."

"How do you know? I only just started calling you that."

Markus and Sigmund could have this kind of conversation for hours. They could maneuver their way into the strangest arguments, which led to the most astonishing conclusions. No one, not even they, could understand how they had become friends. They were as different as night and day, and maybe that was why.

Markus lived in a red wooden house a couple of miles from school. They had moved out there from town two years ago, before his mother died. Now he and his dad lived there alone. He didn't have any brothers or sisters, but he had an amazing autograph collection. Markus was way too nervous to ask famous people for their autographs if he saw them in real life, so he wrote them letters instead. Hundreds of imaginative, well-written, sophisticated, admiring letters. When he was sitting down, bent over a piece of paper with his pencil in his hand, it was like all of his fears disappeared and, strangely, even when the lies were pouring out of him, he would really get into it so that he almost believed what he wrote. Without blushing he could write to a well-known author:

Dear Olav Steingrimsson,

I am sitting in my wheelchair, blinded by tears. I am an 84-year-old widow. Unfortunately I am almost blind and cannot read your poems on my own. But I've had my grandson, little curly-haired Markus Simonsen, read them to me. I must say that they are really good. I used to like Lord Byron best, but now you are definitely my favorite poet. Well, it just so happens that my little Markus collects autographs. It's no exaggeration to say that the boy is the dearest person in the whole world to me. If you, dear Olav Steingrimsson, would consider sending him your autograph, it would warm the heart of both a young man and an old woman. I spent a little of my retirement money to buy an envelope and stamp and hope that you will not disappoint me.

Sincerely, Ms. Aud Simonsen (84 years old)

P.S. Good luck on getting the Nobel Prize—you definitely deserve it!

Or to a famous athlete:

Dear Tormod Jonsen:

Congratulations on becoming the Norwegian national champion. Watching you negotiate the hurdles is like watching a panther leap. Wow, what sheer power! It turns out that at one time I wanted to be a hurdler too. You haven't heard of me because I never made it to the starting line. I bet you want to know why not. The answer is simple: performance-enhancing drugs! And who do you think gave me the drugs?

My parents! They wanted to turn me into an Olympic cham-
pion. Instead they turned me into a wreck. I'll never be able
to clear a hurdle again as long as I live. All I have left are the
autographs of athletes I admire, and that's why I'm writing.
You, Tormod Jonsen, have always been my idol. If you would
send me your autograph, it would be something I could take
out and enjoy when the bitterness threatens to overwhelm
me, which it so often does.

   Yours in athletic appreciation,
   Markus Simonsen (18 years old)
   P.S. Enjoy the Olympic Gold Medal that I'll never have.

He wrote heaps of letters like these, and he almost always got a
response. The walls of his room were covered with pictures of
famous people he had received from around the world, and his
dresser drawers were full of letters with autographs and words of
encouragement. This was a source of enjoyment to both him and
his father, who collected stamps, worked in an office, and was just
as anxious a person as Markus. Really the only difference between
them was their ages; otherwise they were remarkably similar. Same
hair color, same stooped walk, same kind of glasses. The only
difference was that Markus was thin, and Mons Simonsen was fat.
At work they called him the Mole. Markus didn't know that, but
then his dad didn't know that people called him Wormster either.

It started on a field trip. A trip to the mountains that Mr. Skog had
announced one day in Norwegian class, a nice way to end their
sixth-grade year:

"Before you join the ranks of junior high schoolers, where boys learn to become men and girls, women."

"Where they have tits and periods," Reidar mumbled under his breath, but Mr. Skog pretended he hadn't heard because he was a peace-loving man who avoided unpleasantness whenever he could.

"Girls develop faster than boys," Ellen Christine said.

"Well, you sure didn't," Per Espen said contemptuously. "I mean, Reidar's got hair up above *and* down below. None of you have that."

Markus and some of the girls blushed, but Ellen Christine didn't back down. She gave Per Espen a patronizing look and scoffed:

"You have no idea!"

"Isn't that right, Mr. Skog," Per Espen said, "boys are better."

"We develop so differently," Mr. Skog said cautiously.

"Not Reidar!" Per Espen said. "Ow!" He was sitting in the seat in front of the young man with the hair up above and down below, and he jumped up as the tip of a pencil poked into his back.

"When are we going to go?" Sigmund asked.

Markus glanced at him gratefully. He had been sitting with his head hanging over his desk, just waiting for someone to ask him where he had hair.

"The last weekend in May," Mr. Skog said. "I've got a permission slip that you can take home for your parents to sign, and I hope everyone will come."

"As long as no one gets knocked up," Reidar mumbled, but luckily the bell rang right then.

It was Friday afternoon, and there were two hours until the bus would leave from the school parking lot. Both Markus and his father were dreading this trip to the mountains. Mons knew he would spend the three days his son was away in constant fear that Markus would drown in a mountain lake, get lost in the fog, or fall off a cliff. Markus wasn't sure what he was most afraid of, and knowing that his feet were probably going to be covered with blisters was the least of his problems. But both of them pretended they weren't worried. They always did that.

"Are you going to be up high?" Mons asked.

"Yeah," Markus said, "I figure we are."

"Above the tree line?"

"Yeah, way above that, I think."

"Oh, too bad for the student who's afraid of heights then," Mons said bravely.

"Yeah," Markus replied, "too bad."

Markus had never told his father that he was deathly afraid of heights. He'd never had to because Mons was afraid of heights himself, and they had never been up to the mountains or even up in any tall buildings together. They both hid all their anxieties from each other, and since both of them were equally scared, there was no problem. Mons helped Markus pack his backpack until it looked like a little elephant that had overeaten. Mons wiped the sweat off his forehead.

"Well, I think we remembered all the most important stuff."

Markus glanced down at the overstuffed backpack. "Seems like it."

"Let's run through the list," Mons said. "Wool socks, long underwear, regular underwear, shirts, sweaters, scarf, windproof mittens, snowsuit, tracksuit, sneakers, galoshes, rain gear, swimsuit, towel, toothbrush, toothpaste, aspirin, Band-Aids, thermometer, Ace bandage, cod liver oil pills, mosquito netting, camera, Yahtzee … because I'm sure you'll fit in a game of Yahtzee with the boys. You see how well I know you?"

Markus nodded. "Maybe a game or two, yeah."

"Compass, pajamas, sunglasses, spare pair of glasses, SPF 10 suntan lotion, rope …"

"Rope?"

"Yeah, you never know when you'll need some rope when you're up in the mountains. Powdered milk, matches …"

"I don't smoke, Dad."

"I know that, Markus. Just to be on the safe side."

"In case I feel like taking up smoking, after all?"

"In case you need to light a campfire."

"Oh, right."

"Handkerchief, nasal spray, hot chocolate mix, binoculars, sleeping bag, trowel …"

"I'm not going to need a trowel."

"No, I'm sure you won't. But take it along anyway."

"Why?"

"It's a good thing to have. In case you need to dig in."

Markus gave his dad a serious look. "I am totally sure I'm not going to want to dig in, Dad."

"If there's a sudden snowstorm."

"There's not going to be a storm. The teacher said there isn't any snow up there."

"Well, then you don't need a trowel," Mons said, sounding

relieved and giving Markus a playful shove on the chest. "My son, the mountain climber!"

Markus pushed him back. "My old man! "

Although Markus and Mons almost never shared their innermost feelings with each other, they were real pals. If Markus hid his anxiety from Mons, it was just so it wouldn't rub off on him. And the same was true for Mons. The truth was that they had seen through each other a long time ago. They both knew it, and that made the bond between them even stronger.

Mons helped Markus on with his backpack. "Is it heavy?"

Markus staggered a little from side to side before he got his balance. "A little. Maybe you should take out the thermometer."

Mons laughed. "Maybe I should volunteer to go along as your porter."

It sounded like a joke, but Markus knew that he really meant it. He noticed that his body was starting to feel a little numb.

"I don't think so, Dad. I'm growing up, you know."

"Yes, you certainly are."

"With tits and periods."

"What did you say?"

"I mean with hair up above and down below."

"What?"

Markus stood up straight. The backpack weighed at least a ton. He smiled at his dad. "Another time, Dad. We can go camping together in the mountains another time."

"Just the two of us?"

"Yeah, just you and me, Dad, and then we'll climb all the way to the top!"

Mons Simonsen smiled back. Actually, they were both quite sad and they both knew it, but neither of them wanted to say what they were thinking.

"It's a deal," Mons said, giving Markus another playful shove.

The weight of the backpack made him tip over, landing on the ground with a crash. Mons leaned over him. "Markus! Are you OK?"

Markus smiled up at his dad. "*No problemo*, man, but maybe you could help me carry the backpack out to the car?"

CHAPTER 2 Everyone in the school parking lot was in high spirits, and Markus had a strong sense that everyone was staring at him as he and his dad got out of the car. Some of the girls who had been talking the loudest leaned over to each other and started whispering when Mons opened the trunk. Everyone held their breath. Markus shook his head imperceptibly when his dad offered to help him on with his backpack. Mons set it down on the ground and gave Markus a hug.

"Be careful, son."

He said it quietly, but to Markus it sounded like he had bellowed it out.

"I have Mr. Skog's cell phone number," Mons said. "Do you want me to call you tonight and say good night?"

"Don't call us. We'll call you," Markus mumbled.

He didn't turn around when Mons got back in the car, but when the engine started he turned around after all. He waved at the rear windshield and knew that his dad had seen him in the rearview mirror, and he felt his classmates staring at the back of his neck. He bent down over his backpack and heard a low voice somewhere behind him:

"And now an attempt to set the world record for deadlifting."

It didn't work. Markus tried to look as if he were thinking about something else as he squatted down and stuck his arms through the backpack's shoulder straps. When he tried to stand up, it pulled him over backward. He put one knee on the ground, bent his upper body forward, and slowly stood up. His face was beet red. Someone was clapping. He turned around slowly, stared up at the sky, and tried to look as if he were pleased at how nice the weather was. Then he staggered slowly, his legs stiff, over to the bus where the other students were standing. He was the smallest boy in the class, but he had the biggest backpack.

"Did you bring binoculars?" Sigmund asked.

Markus nodded.

"If it's clear tonight, I'll show you the Big Dipper," Sigmund said. "What do you have in your backpack?"

"Just the essentials."

"Are you planning to move up to the mountains for good, Wormster?"

Reidar had come over to them. His backpack looked like it weighed only a couple pounds. Markus shook his head. It felt as if he were being pushed down into the ground. Sigmund gave Reidar a friendly smile.

"So what do you have in your backpack, Reidar? Just a toothbrush and some condoms?"

Reidar tried to come up with a retort and couldn't think of one, so he sneered, walked away, and put his arm around Ellen Christine's shoulders.

"He thinks he's tough, but really he's as cowardly as a crab louse," Sigmund whispered.

"Yeah, that's what I figure," Markus whispered back and let Sigmund help him off with his backpack. Sigmund wasn't Dad, and besides none of it mattered anyway.

They got on the bus, and Markus noticed that Mona had brought her guitar. So, there was going to be a sing-along. And a sing-along meant that he would be forced to do something he absolutely did not want to do, but that was par for the course.

Markus and Sigmund found an empty seat in the middle of the bus.

Trapped on a bus for four hours of mandatory group singing, Markus thought. Surrounded by the enemy.

There were two teachers on the trip, Viktor Skog and Karianne Pedersen. Ms. Pedersen was the school's most popular teacher. She was in her late twenties and held the record time on the local orienteering course. Plus she knew a zillion sing-along songs. Mr. Skog was over forty. He played piano and sang in a chorus. It was going to be a long weekend.

Mona was sitting at the very front of the bus. They had been driving for exactly eight minutes when she opened her guitar case. She started singing:

"A sing-along, a sing-along:
It's something we do all day long!
And if we don't do it all day long,
Then it's not a sing-along.
A sing-along, a sing-along:
It's something we do all day long!"

"A field trip," began Ms. Pedersen, who was sitting in the seat next to Mona, "a field trip,
Is something we find really hip.
And if it isn't really hip,
Then it's not a field trip.

A field trip, a field trip

Is something we find really hip.

Come on, boys and girls, all together now!"

And the boys and the girls all chimed in:

"A field trip, a field trip

Is something we find really hip."

"Your turn, Ellen Christine," Ms. Pedersen called out cheerfully.

"A sunny day, a sunny day," Ellen Christine began.

And they kept going like that, working their way back through the bus. When their turn came, each student would start a verse and then everyone would join in to finish the verse together. They sang about sunny days, chimney sweeps, an athlete, an amusement park, a picture, a little prince, a boy scout, and various other things. Some rhymed, others tried and didn't quite make it, but everyone contributed their little verse. Markus wondered for a second if they had secretly practiced without him. It was going to be his turn soon. He wracked his brains trying to come up with something to sing about, but his mind was like a black hole. He glanced in desperation at Sigmund who was singing:

"A molecule, a molecule,

Is something really miniscule.

And if it isn't miniscule,

Then it's not a molecule.

A molecule, a molecule,

Is something really miniscule."

Markus closed his eyes, sank his head down forward, and started emitting a faint snoring sound. Sigmund nudged his side and said, "Your turn, Wormster." Markus snored louder, but it didn't help. Sigmund pinched his arm. Sigmund was his best friend, but even he didn't always get Markus.

"Come on, Markus!" Ms. Pedersen hollered. She hollered with the best of intentions. She was a simple soul who truly believed that a sing-along would build class spirit so no one would feel left out. She was much too good at things to understand that it could also make the shy students shyer and the lonely students lonelier than they already were.

"An autograph …" Markus sang faintly in a gravelly voice, "an autograph …" Then he froze, utterly silent. There wasn't a word in the world that rhymed with autograph. He closed his eyes.

"Great, Markus," Ms. Pedersen encouraged. That didn't especially cheer him up.

"An autograph," he mumbled hoarsely.

"Exactly!" Ms. Pedersen hollered. "An autograph!"

Markus felt like he was going to faint. "An autograph," he whispered.

Finally Ms. Pedersen understood that he needed help:

"An autograph," she sang, "an autograph …"

But she couldn't find anything to rhyme with autograph either.

"Is just a boring autograph!

And if it's not a boring …"

She smiled down at Markus in encouragement. He had leaned his head against the back of the seat in front of him and wasn't making any noise.

"Autograph!" Sigmund took over. "Then it's just a boring autograph."

"An autograph," everyone chimed in, "an autograph,

Is just a boring autograph!"

So much for that. It could have gone better, but it could have gone worse too. He was still alive, and there were still a lot of people to go before they started the next song.

"A brainless worm," Reidar sang, "a brainless worm,

It cannot think but likes to squirm.

And if it doesn't like to squirm,

Then it's not a brainless worm.

A brainless worm, a brainless worm,

It cannot think but likes to squirm."

Ms. Pedersen and Mr. Skog didn't get why the students were cheering extra loud for the worm verse, but clearly everyone was in a better mood again after the awkward autograph verse, so they joined in and cheered too, and Ms. Pedersen winked at Markus to make sure he felt included in the good mood. Markus blinked his eyes in response to show that everything was all right and to fight back his tears. Then Mr. Skog's cell phone rang. Mona stopped playing.

"Yes, hello? What? Yes, it is. Oh, sure, everything's fine. What? Yes, in a good mood. Yes, I'll tell him."

He closed his cell phone and announced, "That was Markus's dad."

Markus looked out the window and wondered if it opened so he could jump out.

"He called to wish us a good trip!"

Halfhearted applause spread through the bus, Mona started playing again, and Per Espen sang:

"A daddy's boy, a daddy's boy.

He's such a wimp it does annoy!"

Now's a good time to go to sleep, Markus thought. I'll just relax my whole body and then I'll fall asleep. He actually did manage to fall asleep. His head slid down onto Sigmund's shoulder as Sigmund sat there, pondering the mysteries of the stars in the sky.

The class sang their songs, swapped stories about previous camping trips, told jokes, bickered, ate chocolate and potato chips, burped, asked each other riddles, and wondered when they would get there. Markus was somewhere completely different. He was in Hollywood, going from door to door in Beverly Hills collecting autographs. Arnold Schwarzenegger had just invited him in for a glass of vegetable juice when the bus stopped and Mr. Skog announced that they were there now.

CHAPTER 3 It was starting to get dark. The old lodge where they were going to spend the night was two thousand feet above sea level. The next day they would go up to one of the Norwegian Mountain Touring Association cabins, which was up another two thousand two hundred feet. It was more than a four-hour hike, and Markus had decided not to think about it until it was absolutely necessary. He looked up at the mountain: a blue-gray shadow blocking out the evening sun. He could just make out some white blotches way up there. That must be snow or maybe small glaciers with deep crevasses. Whatever it was, he figured it was something unpleasant he was going to have to hike across without even a trowel to dig himself out with in case there was an avalanche. Actually, it wasn't just avalanches he had to be afraid of. What if there was a landslide? Whatever came hurtling down the mountain, be it snow or rock, he was sure that when it happened it would happen right where he was. Something bleated in the distance. Probably wolves in sheep's clothing. He'd heard of that. They were no joke, but then he wasn't planning on joking around at all. He was planning to lie low for the whole trip. Very low. Clinging to the faint hope that he would come down with a fever so he could stay at the lodge the next day, he followed the others to the reception desk, where a very fat, very friendly woman greeted them and told them they would be having fresh mountain trout and prune soup for dinner. The realization that he might get a fish bone stuck in his throat so that he would have to be rushed to a nice, safe hospital perked him up a little bit.

They were divided up into two rooms. The girls and Ms. Pedersen would sleep in the bigger room, the boys and Mr. Skog in the smaller one. It would be crowded, but luckily none of the boys had brought a guitar. Thank goodness. He followed Sigmund into the bedroom and let his backpack drop to the floor with a crash. It sounded like something broke. The thermometer? Then there would be mercury rolling around loose in his pack. That would be terrible. He opened the pack slowly, wondering if a ray of mercury would shoot him in the eye. As far as he knew, mercury was dangerous stuff that could squirt around through the air. But it wasn't the thermometer. It was the mug his mom had given him. The white mug she had painted "Markus" on in red letters. Now it was lying there in three big pieces. There was an M on one, ARK on another, and US on the third piece. He looked at the pieces miserably.

"The world moves from order to disorder," Sigmund said gloomily. "But I think it can be glued," he added when he saw the unhappy expression on Markus's face.

"It doesn't matter," Markus mumbled. "It's a really old mug."

"You can borrow my cup," Sigmund said. "I can use the top of the thermos."

"Almost as old as me," Markus said. "Do you think it's an omen?"

Nine out of ten people would have either laughed at him or asked him what he meant by "omen." But not Sigmund. He understood that Markus meant an omen that soon he might fall apart too, just like the mug did. He stared thoughtfully at the pieces.

"No, I don't think so, but you never know. It's best to be careful," Sigmund said.

"Yeah, that's what I figure," Markus said gloomily and started unrolling his sleeping bag.

Almost all the boys had kind of high-tech looking sleeping bags. Pretty new, but still well used. Clear indications that this was not their first trip to the mountains. Markus had a really old sleeping bag, and it was practically unused. Mons had used it twice during the month he had been a boy scout, almost thirty years ago. It was heavy, gray, a little lumpy, and the zipper was stuck.

"Only mummies sleep in bags like that," said Per Espen, who had gotten a blue Ajungilak-brand sleeping bag for Christmas.

"Yeah? What do you know about mummies, Per Espen?" Sigmund asked. "I mean, apart from what you've learned from comic books?"

Per Espen didn't answer. He was the second shortest boy in the class and knew who he could pick on and who he couldn't.

Markus gave up trying to zip up his sleeping bag and decided to use it as a blanket instead.

"Are we ready, boys?" Mr. Skog asked. "Markus, everything all right over there?"

"Yeah, seems like it," Markus responded.

He didn't get a fish bone stuck in his throat, but he didn't get much trout either. He felt more sick than hungry and didn't eat any more than was absolutely necessary to avoid attracting attention. After the meal everyone gathered in the room with the fireplace, where they received their instructions for the next day. Then, after a quick sing-along, they were told to go to bed.

"It's going to be a long day tomorrow," Mr. Skog said. "It's ten thirty now, and you'll need all the sleep you can get. Ms. Pedersen and I will be up for a little while making plans. We'll be back in half an hour, and we expect the bedrooms to be quiet then."

After eleven complaints, a loud suggestion that they play twenty questions, and a quieter one about strip poker had all been brushed aside, the students said good night and went to brush their teeth and find their sleeping bags. Ms. Pedersen and Mr. Skog each ordered a soda, sat down by the window, and looked out at the mountain they would tackle tomorrow.

"Sharon Stone," Viggo whispered. "Sharon Stone has tits like mountains. She's been in *Playboy*."

"Melanie Griffith is hotter," Per Espen mumbled. "I'd like to have her under the covers, right, Reidar?"

"She's married to Don Johnson," Reidar said. "I don't really want Don Johnson under the covers."

"No, I think they got divorced," Viggo mumbled. "I think Melanie Griffith got together with Antonio Banderas, but they might be divorced now too."

"Almost all of them are divorced," Leif Åge mumbled. "They get married, then they screw, then they get divorced again." Leif Åge's parents had just separated, so he figured he was an expert on divorce.

"Not Diana Mortensen," Sigmund said. "She's never been married."

"That's true," Viggo said. "Diana Mortensen is really picky. But I think she was together with Michael Douglas."

"Everyone's been with Michael Douglas," Reidar said dismissively.

"Not Melanie Griffith," Viggo said. "Because she's with Don Johnson or Antonio Banderas. Unless they're divorced, that is," he added to be on the safe side.

"Paul Newman has never been divorced," Per Espen said. "He's been married the whole time. Just like my mom and dad."

"What do you mean 'the whole time'?" Sigmund asked.

"You know, forever."

"What, like since the Big Bang?"

"What kind of bang?"

"The origin of the universe."

"Knock it off! I meant …"

"I give ten points to Sharon Stone," Viggo said, "and nine points to Diana Mortensen and eight points to …"

And while the boys in class 6B from Ruud Elementary School discussed who the sexiest of Hollywood's single, married, and divorced movie stars were, Markus whispered softly to Sigmund:

"Who's Diana Mortensen?"

"Don't you know?"

"No, but don't tell anyone."

"Diana Mortensen is Norwegian. She's actually from Horten, just south of Oslo, but she lives in Hollywood. She's on *The Rich and the Powerful*."

The Rich and the Powerful was one of those interminable

American soap operas that was shown on Norwegian TV every Wednesday night.

"Haven't you ever seen it?"

"Nope."

"I'm with you there. The show sucks, but it's on right after *The Boundless Universe*. I've seen it a few times."

"Is she … is she pretty?"

"Yeah, she's really pretty. But I don't think she's doing that well."

"Why not?"

"I don't know. She has kind of a sad look in her eyes. Behind all the makeup. I have a picture of her in my wallet."

"Why?"

"I don't know," Sigmund said nonchalantly. "It's pretty much a coincidence."

"Let me see."

"OK, but don't show it to anyone."

Sigmund took out a folded piece of paper and handed it to Markus, who ducked under his sleeping bag and turned on the flashlight he had laid out next to his bag.

Diana Mortensen was sitting on the edge of a swimming pool. Her skin was very pale, her hair was bleached, and her lips were bright red. She was staring out at Markus with big eyes that were as blue as the bikini she was wearing. The photographer had obviously surprised her, because even though her face was turned toward the camera, she was relaxing, leaning back, with her back toward the camera. She was propping herself up on her hands. Her mouth was half open. She was smiling, but at the same time she had a surprised, almost frightened, expression on her face. One of her breasts was showing. On the other side of the pool there was an enormous guy wearing swim trunks. He did not look happy.

Markus swallowed and switched off the flashlight. He took a deep breath and turned the flashlight on again. She was still smiling, but he thought she looked even more afraid than before. Her nipple was small and red. She was probably twenty at the oldest. He felt Sigmund's hand tug on the sleeping bag.

"What are you doing?"

"Nothing."

"Give me the picture."

Markus turned the flashlight off again and handed the picture that Sigmund had coincidentally cut out of a magazine back to its owner.

"I saw her tits."

"Just one of them."

"Yeah," Markus whispered. "Who's the guy on the other side of the pool?"

"Her bodyguard."

Sigmund put the picture back in his wallet and looked over at the others, who were in the middle of a discussion about whether Julia Roberts should get four points or three points. That meant they could continue their conversation undistracted.

"Right after the picture was taken, he tried to destroy the camera, but the photographer was able to get away. When the picture was published, Diana Mortensen sued the photographer."

"Why?"

"She felt like he had invaded her privacy, but she lost."

"So then she doesn't get any privacy?"

"Nope. The court thought she did it on purpose."

"Did what?"

"Sat there half naked like that. The court thought it was a PR stunt, that she had planned it all out in advance."

"But then she wouldn't look so scared, would she?"

"The court thought she was just acting."

"Then the court doesn't know what it's talking about," Markus whispered.

"That's what I think too."

"If I were the judge, I'd have taken away that photographer's right to take pictures for the rest of his life," Markus whispered angrily.

Sigmund nodded in the semidarkness.

"They call her the Norwegian Marilyn Monroe."

"Who's Marilyn Monroe?"

"An actress who lived a long time ago. She was a sex symbol too. She died when she was in her thirties. They don't know if it was murder or suicide. It's a tough world."

"Yeah, that's for sure," Markus replied.

"Time to get some shuteye, boys!"

That was Mr. Skog, who was done drinking his soda and making plans. He crawled into his sleeping bag. Then someone whispered:

"Three points."

"What was that?"

"Three points, teacher."

"What do you mean by that, Reidar?"

"Julia Roberts. I give her three points."

"How nice for Julia Roberts. Now let's get some sleep."

Soon the sound of deep breathing from twelve sleeping boys and one man filled the room, and no one heard a quiet voice under an old-fashioned sleeping bag below the window say:

"Diana Mortensen, ten points."

Diana had fallen asleep by the side of the pool, with her back against the marble tiles and her exposed breasts pointing up toward the red-hot sun. It must hurt to lie like that without a Therm-a-Rest or blanket. Luckily he had brought his new blue Ajungilak sleeping bag. He felt so sorry for her. Because he knew that even though she was world famous, she was really just a scared little sex symbol, who no one understood, except him. He knew exactly how she felt. He was her bodyguard, but also her big brother. He had been little and scared once too. He walked over to her, silently, so as not to wake her. In one quick movement he opened the zipper on the sleeping bag. No problem on a bag like this. Piece of cake. He laid it over her and whispered:

"Have no fear, Diana. I'm here."

A flash of light brighter than the sun exploded in his face. The photographer! That damned photographer who never left them alone.

"Give me that camera!" he growled.

"What's going on?"

Markus was staring down at Mr. Skog's terrified face. He had spread his gray sleeping bag over the teacher and was stroking his cheek.

"Wormster sleepwalks, Mr. Skog."

Reidar had turned on the lights. He was standing over by the door, his face scarlet from pent-up laughter. Markus quickly pulled his hand away from Mr. Skog's cheek.

"Wormster?"

"Uh, I mean Markus, Mr. Skog."

Everyone was awake now. Mr. Skog looked pretty confused.

"I didn't know you walked in your sleep, Markus."

Markus didn't answer. There was only one thing to do: pretend he was still asleep. Slowly, with sleepwalker-like movements, he picked his sleeping bag back up and walked toward the exit.

"Oh, help, a ghost!" Per Espen whispered in delight, but Sigmund put an end to the laughter that had started to spread throughout the room:

"Shhh! Don't wake him up."

"Why not?" Viggo asked. "I mean, he can't walk around like that all night."

"If you wake someone up when they're sleepwalking, it can be a shock to their system."

It got quiet the way it gets quiet when twelve boys simultaneously try not to burst out laughing, without quite succeeding. Markus felt how Sigmund cautiously took hold of his arm and helped him back to his spot.

"Good, Sigmund," Mr. Skog whispered. "We'll just keep our eyes on him for a bit."

"Leave him to me," Sigmund mumbled, helping Markus into his sleeping bag.

"How did you get the zipper unstuck?" he whispered a little later once the others had fallen asleep.

"I dreamt that I just pulled on it," Markus whispered back.

"That's what I thought. Dreams can be just as real as reality."

"Yeah," Markus responded. "That's what I figure."

Four hours later Mr. Skog's alarm clock rang. It was seven thirty in the morning, and Markus had no idea whether he'd slept or not.

CHAPTER 4 "That's quite a narrow bridge, Mr. Skog," Per Espen said.

They were on their way up to the cabin and had reached the first obstacle, a bubbling brook that looked more like a river to Markus. There were big rocks on both sides of the brook that had been worn smooth by the green mountain water.

Nice rocks for slipping on, thought Markus, who actually was in a really good mood. Strangely enough, breakfast had gone without incident. No one had mentioned the episode from the previous night. Sure, maybe some of the girls had given him weird looks, but then they always did that.

One possibility was that maybe Mr. Skog had told them that it could still be a shock to Markus's system if anyone laughed at him because he had been sleepwalking; another was that they were looking forward to the hike so much that they had simply forgotten the whole business.

His backpack was a lot lighter than yesterday. At Sigmund's suggestion he had left the things that were least necessary behind at the lodge. And that was most of it. Of course he was still dreading the hike, but the sense of impending doom was a little less oppressive than it had been the day before.

"That's not a bridge, it's a plank," Mona said. "Me first!" It was easy for Mona. She took gymnastics and was used to the balance beam. Plus she had hiking boots that would stick like glue to even the slipperiest plank. She stepped out onto the plank, jumped up and did the splits, and gracefully landed back on the plank. All of the girls cheered. Markus bit his tongue. He was wearing rubber boots that came up to his knees, and he did not take gymnastics.

He decided not to be the last one to cross the brook, but definitely not the first one either. Number twelve or fourteen, ahead of Sigmund, attracting as little attention as possible, should do the trick.

Reidar took off his boots.

"Teacher, can I wade across?"

"No," Mr. Skog said. "The water is moving pretty fast. You might slip on the rocks."

And be carried away by the current, Markus thought, floating helplessly down toward the waterfall and then farewell, farewell …

Now it was his turn. Cautiously he stepped out onto the plank. It looked as if the brook had been waiting just for him. It was bubbling worse than ever. There was probably some kind of River Demon—who'd been notified that lunch was on its way—ready to come and get him. Sure, well, he might be a little scared, but he was in a good mood, and at least he could kid around with himself during this moment of peril.

Just think about something else, he thought. Think about something else and about where to put your feet at the same time. That was the trick. Three more steps and he would be on solid ground, or unstable rock, depending on how you looked at it.

"You aren't superstitious, are you, Markus?" shouted Per

Espen, who had made it safely across and was very pleased with himself.

Two more steps, Markus thought.

"You're the thirteenth person to go across, you know."

He flung himself forward. The leap of a tiger. A world record in the long jump. He landed on his stomach, clinging to the rock. One of his hands caught on something sharp, and he knew it was going to bleed.

"Why in the world did you do that?" Mr. Skog asked.

"I ... I just felt like jumping."

"You have to be careful, boy."

Markus slowly got up, glancing down at his hand. He was right. A little blood was trickling out of his palm, but it wasn't clear if anyone else had realized that. He noticed that no one was laughing. His classmates were looking at him with something like amazement. As if they were seeing him with new eyes at any rate. He didn't understand why until Ms. Pedersen said, "Well, you're a bit of a wild man, aren't you, Markus?"

"Nah," Markus said, "I just like to jump."

They were above the tree line now. Markus and Sigmund were walking together along the narrow dirt path that stretched like a brown scar up the side of the mountain. There were loose rocks on both sides of the path. They looked as if they had just recently slid down from the top of the mountain above them. But Markus wasn't afraid. He was a wild man now. The death-defying jumper from Ruud, Norway. He had a reputation to protect. Sure, maybe it was false, but a reputation is a reputation all the same. He looked down at the handkerchief he was holding in his hand. The red stain wasn't big, and his hand had stopped bleeding. Mr. Skog was the only one behind them. Making sure nothing happened. So he could relax. Nothing was going to happen as long as Markus didn't turn around and look down. If he did that he would get dizzy, and if he got dizzy then who knew what would happen? But he didn't look down. He looked up. Up, where there was no danger of falling.

"Are you walking in your sleep, Wormster?"

It was Reidar. He was at least one hundred feet farther up when he yelled. The echo was cool. Especially when it answered back: "Sleep, Wormster!"

Now was the time to defend his good reputation before it turned bad again. He lowered his head, clenched his teeth together and started running, off the path, straight up the side of the mountain through the heather. Way in the distance he heard Mr. Skog call out, "Markus!"

And the mountain answered: "Markus!"

He could taste blood in his mouth, but didn't stop. He stared down at the ground as he ran up over a carpet of green, red, purple, pink, white, and yellow. Purple mountain saxifrage and spring pasqueflower, Arctic birch and heather, grass and lichen. He looked up. A huge stone loomed over him like a building. A good stone to climb up onto if you're a wild man who wants to enjoy nature.

"Wait!"

It was Sigmund. Markus started climbing up onto the stone. Catch up with me, he thought. Please catch up with me! Now he was up on the stone. He stood with his back to the valley and his eyes turned upwards. Come on! Please come before I turn around!

"What are you doing, Wormster?"

Sigmund was up on the stone, staring at him, his eyes wide with fright. Markus had never seen him like this before. Only a friend could look like that.

"Please," he panted, "please, don't call me Wormster."

Sigmund put his arm around Markus's shoulders and said, "Never again, Markus."

Markus smiled at him.

"I got all the way up here by myself. Did you see that?"

Sigmund nodded. It looked like he was about to start crying.

"Yeah, I saw it."

"I wanted to see the view, you know. That's why I did it."

"Don't look at it," Sigmund said. "You don't have to."

"And you don't have to understand everything either," Markus whispered. "Not all the time."

"What in the world are you boys doing?"

It was Mr. Skog. He was red and out of breath and not happy.

"Mountains are not something to joke around with. You know full well we all have to stick together."

"That's what we're doing, teacher," Sigmund said and gave Markus's shoulder a light squeeze before removing his arm.

"I just wanted to see the view," Markus said.

"I appreciate that," Mr. Skog said, "but you're going to have to rein in your love for adventure a little."

Markus nodded and Mr. Skog, who did not want to seem strict, winked at him.

"But I do have to concede that the view is wonderful from here. Look how beautiful the spring pasqueflowers are."

"*Pulsatilla vernalis,*" Sigmund said.

"Of course," Mr. Skog said. He had a reputation to protect as well and didn't want the students to know that he didn't know the Latin names of all the wildflowers. "Isn't the pulsatilla lovely, Markus?"

Markus turned around and stared down the mountainside.

"Yeah," he mumbled as he sank down onto the rock, then lay down, staring up at the sky that was spinning above him. "The pulsatilla is lovely."

A man and a woman in their twenties were sitting outside the wall of the cabin. They had nut-brown faces with chalk-white teeth and broad smiles. They looked as if they had stepped out of a mountain-climbing ad. The man was calmly smoking a pipe and studying a map. The woman was just sunning herself. Markus wondered if they owned the cabin, but when they opened their mouths they started speaking Danish and explained that they were tourists who were planning to go up to the glacier.

"Oh, teacher, can't we go up there too?" Mona asked.

"No," Mr. Skog said. "I think we've done enough hiking for today. First we'll have something to eat, and then Ms. Pedersen and I will set up a nature trail for you. Then we can divide you into groups to compete. The winner will be the group that finds and correctly identifies the largest number of species on the trail."

"Nature trails are for kindergarteners," Reidar mumbled. "Exploring glaciers is much cooler."

"And more dangerous," Ms. Pedersen said.

"My uncle has gone glacier hiking at least a thousand times," Per Espen said. "He says it's really awesome."

"But not you, Per Espen," Ms. Pedersen said. "You haven't been glacier hiking."

"No," Per Espen said, "but I really want to."

"You'll have to wait until you're older," Mr. Skog said.

Markus didn't know if it was because the mountain air was making him dizzy, or because he was so relieved to have finally made it up here without anyone (except Sigmund) discovering his fear of heights, or just because he was an idiot, but at any rate he said the dumbest thing he could ever say. He didn't want to say it. It just tumbled out of his mouth like an avalanche he couldn't prevent.

"I've been glacier hiking," he said so loudly that everyone, including the Danes, heard him.

"You have, Markus?" Mr. Skog said, a little surprised. "Well, then you know it's no joke."

Markus really wanted to be quiet now, but the avalanche kept going.

"Yeah, you have to be quite an experienced hiker. Otherwise it doesn't go well."

"You're lying," Per Espen said.

"If you've been glacier hiking then I'm skiing legend Vegard Ulvang," Viggo said.

"Dad and I go glacier hiking every summer," Markus said as he tried to swallow his tongue.

"How nice, Markus," Ms. Pedersen said. "Then maybe you can give us a little presentation."

"Presentation?"

"Yes, about glacier hiking."

"Um, when?"

"Tonight," Ellen Christine said. "Before the sing-along."

"That's a great idea," Mr. Skog said.

Markus wanted to say that he needed time to prepare, but the skeptical looks from his suspicious classmates forced the avalanche to continue.

"That would be fine," he said. "I can tell you a bit about my experiences."

"Then that's settled," Mr. Skog said, nodded to the Danes, and walked into the cabin.

It wasn't as big as the lodge further down the mountain. There was no fat, happy woman who served trout and prune soup, just a kitchen cupboard full of canned goods, soda, and chocolate that you could pay for by putting money into a tin can that was hanging on the wall. In addition there was an old-fashioned stove and a box of firewood, and behind the cabin there was a creek where they could fetch fresh, ice-cold mountain water in a bucket that sat against the wall. The path continued on past the cabin, over brown dirt and patches of snow, up to the glacier that sat like a blue-green heaven made of ice, way up there.

They did the nature trail in groups of four. Markus's group won by a huge margin thanks to Sigmund, who knew both the Norwegian and the Latin names of all types of lichen and flowers: Arctic lichen, elegant sunburst lichen, bloodspot lichen, ragged snow lichen, lousewort, fir clubmoss, and all kinds of other stuff. Knowing that before the day was up he would have to give his presentation on glacier hiking made it impossible for Markus to enjoy the victory. There were still a few hours before he was supposed to start, and the time was passing astonishingly quickly and slowly at the same time. Every second was like an eternity, but every hour was like a second.

Mr. Skog set his coffee cup down on the big wooden table.

"All right, everyone," he said. "I'm sure Markus would like to get started now."

An expectant hush fell over the cabin.

"Go right ahead," Mr. Skog said.

Markus stood up. He swayed a little bit and felt his tongue swelling in his mouth.

"Glacier hiking," he began, "is, um ... hiking on a glacier."

He stopped and stared at his classmates in desperation. Some of them had brought paper and pencils to take notes; others were just sitting there sure that he was going to make such an utter fool of himself that he would set the world record for fool-making. Neither Mr. Skog nor Ms. Pedersen understood what was going on. Of course, they thought he was a tough little wild man and an experienced hiker. Why wouldn't they think that? They'd wondered for a long time what was going on inside the shy boy who hardly ever said anything in class. The idea that he was really an experienced glacier explorer confirmed their theory that there are hidden qualities in everyone.

"When you go glacier hiking, it's important to dress warmly."

Sigmund coughed. Was that a secret signal? Had he said something wrong?

"If it's not sunny," he added slowly. "If the sun's out, then dressing warmly isn't that important."

"What about rubber boots that come up to your knees?" Reidar muttered.

Someone giggled. It was probably Ellen Christine.

"With spikes," Markus whispered. "Rubber boots with spikes."

Per Espen's laughter was what started the whole thing. The words started pouring out of Markus's mouth, at first stammered and disjointed:

"When Dad and I went glacier hiking last year … it was … very cold … It was so windy that there was … that there was a hurricane."

Someone whistled. He knew that was a warning sign, but he didn't care. He was on a roll.

"Yeah," he said loudly. "It was actually a major hurricane!"

"A major hurricane?" Mona whispered.

Markus kept going.

"Dad and I were looking out over the glacier. It was getting really serious. The fog was coming in …"

"What was the fog doing?" Viggo asked.

"It was coming in, so it was getting hard to see!"

"That's what I thought," said Viggo, who was one of the ones taking notes.

"Shh!" Mr. Skog said.

"The fog was coming in and it was getting hard to see," Markus continued. "Snow had filled in the ski tracks behind us. What were we going to do? Should we turn back?"

"No!" four boys and three girls all yelled at the same time.

"No!" Markus yelled back. "We … we didn't turn back! We just kept going! We kept going on our glacier hike!"

He tried to stop, but he couldn't. The words were coming faster and faster. He had no idea what he was saying. It wasn't him talking. It was all happening on its own, burying his thoughts in a terrible avalanche of wild, imagined events and crazy lies.

"The warm cabin was waiting for us on the other side of the mountain. That was what saved us. We leaned into the wind and kept going. The glacier was as slippery as an ice-skating rink!"

He took a breath. It was dead quiet in the room. Then the door opened. The Danes had come back. Exhausted, but happy. No problem, let them come! Two more people in the audience wouldn't make any difference.

"So we spread our jackets out and sailed across the glacier with the wind at our backs, cheering and laughing. It was a wonderful day on the mountain."

He could do this. This was just like writing a letter asking for someone's autograph. It all came naturally. He just had to let it happen.

"Hiking on a glacier can be dangerous. Of course everyone knows that. And the most dangerous part of glacier hiking is when there are crevasses in the glacier. Yes, the crevasses are the glacier hiker's worst enemy. And what did we see way up ahead of us?"

"A crevasse," Per Espen whispered hoarsely.

"Yes!" Markus yelled. "A crevasse that was so deep that it was … incredibly deep! And Dad and I were sliding right toward the crevasse!" Then he made a squealing noise, like a car slamming on its brakes. He didn't exactly know why he made the squealing noise. It kind of didn't fit in. But that didn't matter now.

"Yes," he yelled. He made the squealing noise again. "Now it was really getting serious. Again. I weigh less than Dad, so I was going faster. I was sliding really fast. The crevasse was getting closer and closer." He made the squealing noise again. "I thought my final hour had come, but then ... then I heard skating noises behind me. It was Dad. He used to do a lot of ice-skating, you know. Boy, did that come in handy now. I tried to brake, but the major hurricane had grown into a ... super-hurricane! I closed my eyes, and right when I thought my final hour had come, Dad grabbed hold of my backpack. I felt myself being yanked backward, pulled by his massive muscles. But we were still rolling toward the crevasse, and then finally we came to a stop just two feet away from the edge of the black hole!"

Markus closed his mouth. His ears were ringing. It was like he'd given his presentation in the middle of a dream. The floor was moving under his feet. It's just me, walking in my sleep, he thought. Don't wake up now. That could be a shock to my system.

He opened his mouth. No more words came. He stared at the faces around him. They were frozen, turned to ice. Now the ice started to melt. Don't melt, he thought. Please. Don't melt!

"Then what happened?" asked the Danish lady, who was the first to melt.

"Then we went home," Markus said quietly. "And afterward ... we agreed that we'd had a nice time."

Then Mr. Skog's cell phone rang.

"It's your father, Markus," he said slowly. "He's wondering how you're doing."

"I'm doing fine," Markus said and fainted.

There was an extra bedroom in the cabin. Actually, the Danes had been planning on sleeping there, but they had let Markus have it. They decided to sleep in the living room with everyone else, packed together like sardines. No one had made fun of him. Everyone was completely quiet when Mr. Skog led him into the bedroom. He thought that was strange. The more he made a fool of himself, the less they made fun of him. Hmm, maybe they thought he was crazy. Crazy people could be dangerous. And maybe he was too. That must be it. Completely insane, unpredictable and extremely dangerous. A ticking bomb that could go off at any time. He stared at the ceiling and started counting the cracks in the rafters. There were a lot of cracks and the number was sure to keep growing as the years went by. Eventually the roof would probably collapse. That could happen tonight. While he was asleep. "The world moves from order to disorder," Sigmund had said, and Sigmund didn't usually lie. He was the one that did that. But he didn't do it on purpose, just to survive.

"Thirty-one," he counted, "thirty-two, thirty-three."

The door opened. He closed his eyes and snored.

"Markus!" It was Sigmund. "How's it going?"

Markus opened his eyes. "Fine."

"You don't have to lie to me."

"Do you think dreaming is the same as lying?"

Sigmund looked at him a little uncertainly. "I don't know. I guess that depends on what you're dreaming."

"I'm dreaming that everything is different."

"Then it's not lying. Then it's hoping."

"You're so wise, Sigmund."

"Yeah," Sigmund said seriously. "Sometimes I think I might be a genius."

"And you brag just as much as I do."

"I'm not bragging. It's a fact."

"So am I, unfortunately."

"Huh? So are you *what*?"

"A fact. Do you think the roof is going to fall down on my head overnight?"

"No," Sigmund said. "I don't think so." He walked over to the window and looked out. "I can see Sirius, the Dog Star."

"Where?"

"There. The really bright star. But the light we're seeing isn't being emitted now. It's taken more than eight years to get here. What we're seeing is Sirius from a long time ago."

"I wish I were there now," Markus said.

"Where?"

"On Sirius. A long time ago. Are they asleep?"

"Yes."

"I bet they're dreaming about me."

"Why?"

"I thought I heard someone laughing."

"It's stupid to feel sorry for yourself."

"It's stupid to laugh too."

"I'm not laughing," Sigmund said.

"No," Markus said. "But that's just because you're a genius."

He went back and lay down on the bunk bed. Sigmund walked over to the door. Just as he was about to leave, he turned around.

"Is there anything I can do for you?"

"You can destroy Mr. Skog's cell phone."

"I can't do *that*."

"Then you can get me Diana Mortensen's address."

"Why?"

"No reason. I was just wondering where she lives. Do you have it?"

"Yeah, it's under the picture so that her fans can write to her."

"I'm a fan," Markus said.

Sigmund nodded.

"Me too. Coincidentally."

Dear Diana Mortensen!

I'm a Norwegian mountain climber and a millionaire. Currently I'm lying, alone, in a cabin up in the breathtaking alpine wilderness, having just climbed my way out of a crevasse I was so unlucky as to fall into. I got frostbite on a couple of my toes, broke a couple of ribs, and got a few scrapes here and there, but otherwise I'm in great shape. I called the Red Cross on my cell phone and figure help will be here in a few hours. The reason I'm writing is that I found a magazine here in the cabin, and in the magazine I read about the terrible predicament you've wound up in. I just have to tell you that I feel for you. If I'd been your bodyguard, I would have thrown the photographer down into the nearest glacial crevasse. I want you to know that there are lots of mountain-climbing Norwegians who are thinking about you, feeling bad for you, and wishing you all the best. Since I happen to be writing, I want to confide in you that I have a special hobby. As it so happens, I collect autographs. Well, maybe you think that's odd, but as a millionaire I meet so many interesting people. Collecting autographs is an interesting hobby for a lonely millionaire. I am not currently married. The mountains and my business obligations take all my time. I am, you see, a lonely millionaire just as you are a lonely movie star. I can see it in your eyes. But have no fear, Diana Mortensen. Someday we'll both meet the right person, both of us.

With sincere greetings from the wild mountains of Norway,

Markus Simonsen, millionaire

P.S. If you think this letter is a little strange and childish, well that's probably just because I have a mild concussion from when I fell down into the crevasse. Oddly enough, it's making me feel like a kid! I'm sure you can tell that from what I've written and from my handwriting!

When he woke up, he was still holding the pen in his hand. The letter had fallen down onto the floor. He picked it up and put it in an envelope without rereading it. If he did that he would just start second-guessing himself. He would mail it when they got back down to the lodge.

The trip down was worse than the trip up. Because now he had no choice but to look down. He took short steps, his legs stiff and his head down, keeping his eyes trained on the ground. One yard ahead. If only he could have kept his eyes closed, he would have. When he got down, he picked up his things, mailed the letter, and got onto the bus with everyone else. He sat there in silence, listening to the sing-along. He had a bad reputation and cramps in both legs. He wished he could go to Sirius and dreaded the rest of his life.

CHAPTER 5 There was only one week left until summer vacation, but Markus refused to go to school.

"I feel a little feverish," he said.

"We have to call the doctor right away," Mons said, staring in horror at the thermometer, which Markus had heated to 107.6 degrees.

"You don't have to do that," Markus said. "It's just a slight fever."

"Yes, I'm sure it will be fine, you'll see," his father said, dashing out to the phone.

When the doctor came, Markus's fever was down to 98.4.

"The boy is fit as a fiddle," he said. "There must be something wrong with the thermometer."

"Let's hope so," Markus mumbled, smiling weakly at his father.

The doctor left and Markus started pulling his shirt back on. His father was looking at him with concern.

"How are you doing, son?"

"Fine," Markus said, settling back into the bed again. "I'm just a little dizzy."

"I'll drive you to school."

"You don't have to do that, Dad. I'm sure I won't faint until the heat of the classroom hits me."

"You really don't want to go to school, do you, Markus?"

"No, Dad, never."

"Why not?"

They looked at each other for four endless seconds, and Markus knew he didn't have to say anything. Mons ran his hand a little clumsily over Markus's hair.

"I'm sure everything will work out, you'll see."

"When?"

"Eventually."

"No, Dad, eventually it's going to get really bad."

Mons looked at his son sadly. He really wanted to say something encouraging, but he couldn't think of anything.

"I shouldn't have called, should I?" he asked quietly.

"It doesn't matter."

"Did they tease you because I called?"

"No. You called because they tease me."

In his pocket Mons ran his fingers over the cigarettes that he had given up smoking six months before.

"What do you want me to do, Markus?"

"Stay here with me, Dad."

Mons was the one who started crying.

"It'll be all right, Dad," Markus said softly. "After all, *you're* here."

"I have to go to work."

"Call them and say you have … ringing in your ears."

"How did you know that?"

"I guessed," Markus said. "Do you want to play Yahtzee?"

—

Sigmund came over at six thirty to find out how he was doing. Markus said that he was doing great. He'd just had to stay home to take care of his father, who had had a severe attack of ringing in the ears. Sigmund nodded somberly.

"I hope they don't have to poke a hole in your eardrum, Mr. Simonsen," he said.

Mons said that he was feeling much better now and that he was sure Markus would be able to go to school tomorrow.

"We'll cross that bridge when we come to it," Markus said. "Can we have a bowl of ice cream, Dad?"

"You can have two."

"Thanks, Mr. Simonsen," Sigmund said. "Does your eyesight flicker when your ears ring?"

"No, no flickering."

"Because if you see flickering, you should go to the doctor."

"I don't think there needs to be any more discussion of my ears now," said Mons, who for a second thought that his vision was flickering like crazy; but then he realized that he didn't have any ringing in his ears. At least as long as no one was talking about it. He asked, "So, Sigmund, how are things going at school?"

"Well, thanks for asking. It would appear that the youngsters are enjoying themselves, Mr. Simonsen."

Mons looked at Sigmund a little hesitantly. He really wasn't sure if the kid was making fun of him or not, but Markus had said that that was just the way he was. Sigmund always made Mons feel a little insecure, but he reassured himself with the thought that maybe that was precisely the kind of friend Markus needed.

"I'll get the ice cream," he mumbled, heading for the kitchen.

"I got into a fight today," Sigmund said, smiling at Markus.

"With who?"

"Reidar."

"Thanks."

"No need to thank me. Reidar started it."

"Oh?"

"He called me Mini-Professor."

"That's bad."

"Yeah, but I told the principal on him."

"That's good."

"Yeah, I'm not going to stand for any of that."

"Me neither," Markus said.

"Would you like to stay for dinner, Sigmund?" asked Mons, walking back in from the kitchen.

"Thanks, Mr. Simonsen. *The Boundless Universe* is on TV tonight. It's a good show."

"Yes, I'm sure it is," Mons mumbled, handing each of them a bowl of chocolate ice cream.

"Thanks, Mr. Simonsen," Sigmund said. "Chocolate ice cream is good too."

"Too?"

"Yeah, if you don't have strawberry on hand."

"But I do," said Mons, who was starting to get a little irritated. "I have strawberry … in the freezer. I can go get you some of that instead if you want."

"You don't have to do that, Mr. Simonsen. I was just kidding around."

"You kid around a lot, don't you, Sigmund?"

"I get by," Sigmund said, pushing his spoon down into the chocolate ice cream.

They all sat next to each other on the sofa while they watched *The Boundless Universe* and ate dinner. Sigmund took notes. Mons tried to pretend he knew most of it already, and Markus waited impatiently for the next show.

"Well, so much for that," Mons said, getting up to turn off the TV. "What do you say we play a little Yahtzee before Sigmund leaves?"

"What do you say we take a look at the next show, Mr. Simonsen?" Sigmund asked.

"And what show is that? *The Secret of Saturn's Rings?*"

"No, Dad," Markus said. "It's a series: *The Rich and the Powerful.*"

"It's really awful, but sometimes it's interesting to watch something bad," Sigmund said. "I'll call home and ask if I can watch it over here."

The Rich and the Powerful was about two extremely wealthy families locked in competition against each other for ultimate control of every aspect of the construction industry in the United States. They were showing episode 34 tonight. It was unbelievable that Mons had somehow managed to miss the series; it seemed like everyone in Norway was watching it. But the truth was that he hadn't missed it. He had been following it enthusiastically without saying a word to Markus, who never watched TV after nine p.m. except on Saturdays.

Episode 34 was about the race to get a building permit for the world's tallest skyscraper, which was going to be built in New

York City. There was no limit to the dastardly methods the Smith and Jones families used to try to get the job: extortion, bribery, robbery, forgery, kidnapping, rape, and murder. *The Rich and the Powerful* had it all. All of the characters were villains, except for two. And those two were so nice that it was ridiculous. Plus they were in love with each other, a star-crossed love that had a lot of obstacles to overcome. One of the two was Henry, a law student and the youngest son of the Smith family. He was played by Billy Parker, a young Hollywood star with a drinking problem. But that was in the real world. In *The Rich and the Powerful* he never drank anything stronger than tea. The other was Rebecca Jones. She was an only child and, against the wishes of her family, she was going to nursing school. What no one, except for Mrs. Smith and Mrs. Jones, knew was that she was adopted. You see, Mrs. Smith had once had an affair with stockbroker Florian Symms. She got pregnant and made a deal with Mrs. Jones, who wasn't able to have children and who had been her friend at that time, that she would buy the baby after it was born. When Rebecca was born, Mrs. Smith bribed the midwife at the hospital to say that the baby had been stillborn. Then she brought it to Mrs. Jones, who happened to be a patient in an alcohol treatment center right then. When Mrs. Jones went home, she brought Rebecca with her and joyfully told her husband about the surprise birth. That meant that Henry and Rebecca were half-siblings, which was revealed after the terrible accident in episode 41.

Rebecca Jones was played by Diana Mortensen. She looked even younger than in the picture, but then she couldn't have been more than eighteen in episode 34. Markus figured he wasn't going to get to see any tits in *The Rich and the Powerful*. He was right. When you thought about it that was weird, because the characters were sleeping with each other all the time. The old ones, the young ones, in just about every conceivable combination. Kiss, caress, and then full speed ahead into the bedroom. Beautiful music, naked thighs, excited facial expressions, pink sheets moving up and down, but no tits. Sigmund had explained that when Americans had sex on TV, it was exactly like when they drank alcohol on the street. They could guzzle down as much as they wanted as long as they hid the bottle in a paper bag. Everything was allowed as long as it was hidden. In *The Rich and the Powerful* they had a drink as soon as they walked into a room, and they had sex with each other left and right, but you could only guess at how they did it. Which wasn't that hard.

The one character that didn't drink or have sex with anyone was Diana Mortensen's. She mostly walked around and looked sad when she wasn't taking care of the old and the sick. Then she looked happy, stroked their hair, and gave them words of encouragement. But whenever she left the room and was alone, she looked sad again. Markus wasn't exactly sure if that was because she felt bad for all the old people and the sick people, or because her life was so terrible since she was the only one who didn't get to sleep with anyone, at least not her half-brother who she was in love with. If she had wanted to sleep with anyone else, it hadn't worked out. Markus was sure of that. There was no shortage of offers, but when they came Diana Mortensen blushed and chewed out the person who'd asked, before storming off and looking sadder than ever.

Markus had never seen anyone who looked more beautiful when she blushed than Diana Mortensen, and it didn't seem like she was embarrassed about it either. She blushed right in their faces, and then *they* apologized to *her*. They would apologize because she blushed. He'd never seen anything like it. No one ever apologized when *he* blushed. Quite the contrary. They laughed at him. But no one laughed at Diana Mortensen. She would've really let them have it if they had. Because she had a temper too. Yes, Mr. Jones, who thought he was her father, called her a "damned wildcat." What a nickname! Wildcat! He would love to be called that. Markus the Wildcat! Wouldn't that be something? But no one was ever going to call him wildcat. They wouldn't even call him housecat. He was Wormster. Forever.

"Well, what a lame show," Mons said after he turned off the TV.

"I warned you, Mr. Simonsen," Sigmund said.

"I mean, you can guess everything that's going to happen," Mons continued. "The Smith family is going to get the building permit and then …"

Sigmund shook his head.

"No, the Jones family is going to get the permit."

"How do you know that?"

"All the signs are pointing in that direction, Mr. Simonsen."

"I think Diana Mortensen is going to get the building permit," Markus said, "and then she'll give it to the old and the sick."

Both his dad and Sigmund smiled at him a little pityingly.

"Unfortunately, my boy," Mons said, "things like that don't happen in real life, just in imaginary stories."

"But this is an imaginary story, Dad."

Mons looked at the clock and yawned. "Well, boys, I think it's time for bed now."

"How are you doing with the ringing in your ears, Mr. Simonsen?"

After assuring Sigmund that his ears were fine, seeing him out, and saying good night to his son, Mons went to bed. He fell asleep right away and dreamed that a precocious thirteen-year-old doctor was poking holes in both of his eardrums. In the room next door, his son dreamed about a close friendship between a wildcat and a worm.

CHAPTER 6 To his surprise Markus survived his final week at Ruud Elementary School. Sure, people did tease him now and then and ask him which glacier he and his dad were going to climb this summer. He'd blushed probably thirteen or fourteen times, and when he walked back and forth across the playground with Sigmund he moved just as slowly and kept his head just as bowed as before, but he'd made it through relatively unscathed. Maybe it was because he was off in his own world. A world where the rich and powerful reigned and where he had experienced his first great love—for Rebecca Jones, who wasn't Rebecca Jones, but movie star Diana Mortensen in disguise—and where he wasn't the shortest, most fearful boy in the class, but the renowned millionaire and mountain climber, Markus Simonsen, a.k.a. the Wildcat.

Over the course of the week he had starred in no fewer than nineteen episodes of *The Rich and the Powerful*, episodes in which *he* was the hero and Diana Mortensen the heroine. By the time the school bell rang for the last time and summer was here, Diana had broken up with Henry and was going to secretly marry Markus.

Sigmund, for his part, had also had an eventful week. He had told four girls that he was too young to be tied down, gotten into another fight with Reidar, given a present, and made a thought-provoking end-of-the-year speech in honor of Mr. Skog.

"For those of us who are young today," he had said, "six years is a long time. But what is time, really? The poet Gunnar Reiss-Andersen said it this way, 'Time is a distance in a bewitched space.' That's how we want you to remember us, Mr. Skog. No matter how far the distance between us is, remember that we are still in the same room. The room where you drew on your knowledge to make it possible for us to become the members of society we are going to become. In time. And so, please accept this alarm clock. And when it goes off, don't ask: 'For whom does the bell toll?' This bell tolls for you."

This was a very powerful speech, even for Sigmund, and when Markus asked how in the world he had managed to write it, Sigmund confided that he had had some help from his dad.

"But don't tell anyone. They think this is how I am."

"This isn't how you are?" Markus had asked, and Sigmund had given him a serious look and responded, "No, actually I'm a completely normal boy."

Six long years were over, and two completely normal boys walked slowly out of the front door of the school for the last time. They stopped on the steps, looked at each other for a second, and then Markus lifted his head up and yelled, loudly enough for two hundred students and fourteen teachers to hear, "Yippee!"

"A letter came for you," Mons said.

"It's over," Markus said. "I'm free! I'm going to have fourteen pieces of toast with strawberry jam, eleven glasses of chocolate milk, and sixteen scoops of ice cream!"

"From the United States," Mons said. "I didn't know you had a pen pal in America, Markus."

Markus, who was on his way to the kitchen to clean out the fridge, stopped.

"Huh?"

"Here it is. There's no return address on the envelope. Who do you think it's from?"

"I think it's from America," Markus said, knowing that he was blushing more than he had ever blushed in his whole life.

He grabbed the letter and dashed into his room, where he opened it, looked at the signature, tripped over a chair, and got up again without even noticing if it hurt or not.

"Should I make you some food?" his dad hollered.

"I'm not hungry," Markus tried to call back. It sounded more like a groan.

Someone in the living room said, "Man does not live by mail alone," but Markus didn't hear it.

There was no doubt about it. Diana Mortensen was smiling at him from the picture that had been in the envelope along with the letter. He was breathing like a steam engine as he read:

Dear Markus Simonsen:

I'm writing to thank you for your letter. I get quite a bit of mail—fan mail from kids, obscene mail from old pigs, and mail from people proposing to me. (Can you imagine? Mail proposing to little old me!!!) But your letter really stood out. Not just because it came from the Old Country, and because I love Norway's alpine wilderness, but also because I could read between the lines that you are one of the few people who understands me. Yes, I am indeed lonely, but few people know that. Most people think I'm stiff and cold, but deep in my heart I'm still the little girl who, with rosy cheeks and full of expectation, left my mom and dad and all my friends behind and set out to conquer Hollywood and the world. Yes, my dear Markus Simonsen. I am Cinderella, but where is my prince? Who has the other glass slipper? Once more, thank you so much for your letter. I was touched.

Sincerely,

Diana Mortensen

P.S. I've included a picture and the autograph you requested. I'm sure you'll get married someday, but no one knows better than me how difficult it is to find the right person. There's so much I would have liked to write, but I have an appointment with my hairdresser in half an hour. I'll have to leave it at this: My closest friends say that I have a good sense of humor, and my favorite author is William Shakespeare. I dream of being in Romeo and Juliet. *Imagine that, silly old me as Juliet! Once again, thank you.*

Diana

"Here are five of the pieces of toast you ordered," said Mons, who had walked in the door late enough to have just missed seeing Markus put the letter and picture in his pocket. "I can make the other eleven for you when you're done eating these, if you ... Is something wrong, Markus?"

Markus was sitting on the edge of his bed, stiff as a board. He wasn't red in the face anymore; he was quite pale. His eyes were wide, and he was lost in thought and breathing funny.

"No," Markus whispered. "Nothing's wrong."

He cleared his throat and tried to make his voice sound normal.

"Everything's going great. Actually."

To emphasize that everything was normal, he added:

"And how are things going with you, Dad?"

He had tried to make his voice sound completely normal, but it switched into falsetto without his being able to do anything about it. Mons looked at him in surprise, and Markus smiled wanly.

"I'm pretty sure my voice is starting to change, yup," he squeaked. "Well, I'd better be on my way."

He walked slowly toward the door while trying to whistle. It sounded like a goose hissing.

"Where are you going?"

"Oh, I thought I would take a little walk."

"What about the food?"

He looked at his dad in confusion, repeating, "Food?"

"Yeah, the toast I made you. Aren't you going to eat it?"

"Right," Markus said, trying to smile lightheartedly. "I totally forgot about the food. How 'bout that? Ha, ha!"

He took the five pieces of toast off the plate, stacked them one on top of the other, and squashed them together into one giant, gooey sandwich. The jam was oozing out between his fingers.

"I love a nice, thick sandwich," he explained and slipped out the door.

—

Sigmund lived a little further down in the housing development. He was biking up the street now and ran into Markus halfway between their two houses. Without arranging anything in advance, the two of them had set off to see each other at the same time. That happened all the time. Sigmund felt that it was a result of the fact that they were both on the same cosmic wavelength. Without even being aware of it, they had arranged to meet by sending electrical vibrations to each other. "You and me," he'd said, "we don't need the phone. Just thinking about each other is enough."

He stopped his bike and waited for Markus, who came rushing toward him in a frenzy of excitement.

"Hi," Sigmund said calmly. "I thought I'd run into you here."

Markus didn't actually believe Sigmund about the cosmic wavelength stuff. It frequently happened that they didn't meet at the halfway point, and when they did, it was just because they visited each other so often. But then again he wasn't sure; you could never be sure with Sigmund. If anyone was crammed full of cosmic waves, it was bound to be him.

"I got a letter," he panted.

"Very interesting," Sigmund said. "I was wondering if you wanted to go swimming."

"From Diana Mortensen! I got a letter from Diana Mortensen, a really long one!"

For once in his life, Sigmund was speechless.

"Can you believe it! She wrote about all kinds of stuff, about how she's doing … that she is actually really lonely … that she likes the outdoors … that she dreams of playing Julie in Shakespeare, and stuff like that."

Sigmund had finally regained the power of speech.

"Juliet," he said.

"Huh?"

"You mean Juliet. Juliet in *Romeo and Juliet*."

"Yeah, right," said Markus, who had already forgotten the whole Shakespeare thing and had moved, full speed ahead, on to his next thought.

"I wonder if I'm not on the same comic wavelength as Diana Mortensen too, actually."

Sigmund had many good properties. One of his bad ones was that he was uncomfortable whenever he wasn't in control of the situation. Whenever he felt like someone else was in control of the situation, he tried to cover this up by becoming cynical, sarcastic, and snooty. And he definitely wasn't in control of the situation now.

"The word is actually 'cosmic,' Simonsen," he said rather condescendingly.

"Why are you calling me Simonsen?" asked Markus, who hadn't noticed that his friend was struggling desperately to regain control of the situation.

Sigmund gave up.

"But, Markus … why … I mean, why …?"

"Why did she write to me?"

Sigmund nodded in silence, and the person who was really in control of the situation started to explain.

When he'd finished he handed the letter from Diana Mortensen to Sigmund, who read it without saying a word and without giving a thought to who was or wasn't in control of the situation. He folded the letter back up, gave it to Markus, and looked at him with new eyes.

"Sheesh!" he said

"She thinks I'm a millionaire," Markus said.

Sigmund nodded. And giggled. Markus had never heard him do that before. He thought only girls giggled, but it wasn't a snide giggle, it was a nice giggle indicating that they were both in on a secret. An incredible secret that only they knew about. Then he giggled too.

"What are we going to do?"

Sigmund regained his composure as he thought about it.

"I don't know ..." he said slowly, "yet. I suggest that we go swimming. I think best when my body is submerged in water."

Neither of them said anything as Sigmund bicycled, with Markus perched on the rack over the rear tire, along the path through the woods that led down to the little cove where Sigmund liked to dive off the rocks along the shore while Markus waded around in the shallow water collecting seashells. It wasn't that he couldn't swim, he just didn't like to. He had a somewhat unique swimming style. He slowed himself down with his arms while he tried to speed himself up by kicking with his legs. In addition to that, he wasn't particularly excited about the ocean. Watching *Jaws 2* on video had been a serious shock, and the ocean was certainly full of crabs, stinging jellyfish, and eels. He had seen an electric eel at the aquarium in Bergen, and was convinced that if there was an electric eel in Ruud Cove, he was sure to encounter it. Sooner or later. Probably sooner.

There were a lot of people on the beach. Some were sunbathing, some building sandcastles, some running into the water and back out again over and over again while yelling and splashing water on the ones who were sunbathing, some swimming around, some diving down under the people who were swimming and grabbing their legs and pulling them under. Reidar and Ellen Christine were standing in the shallows and tossing a ball back and forth between them. Reidar waved at them when they got there.

"You took a wrong turn, Wormster. There aren't any glaciers here!"

For some reason or other Ellen Christine was pretending that she didn't see them.

"She's crazy about me," Sigmund said. "It's getting a little old. Let's go over to Persvika instead."

Persvika was a smaller cove that was a little further away. The swimming wasn't as good there because the bottom was really rocky; but on the other hand you could have some peace and quiet, plus there was a rock that Sigmund liked to dive off.

Markus sat on the rock with his knees pulled up under him and watched Sigmund, who was swimming toward him with long, steady strokes. He took out the letter and read it one more time. It was almost better than the last time he read it. So open and honest. A person in need. He glanced out at the water. Sigmund wasn't there.

Help, Markus thought, he's drowning! He was just about to call for help, when his friend's head came up out of the water, right below the rock.

"You have to write to her," Sigmund said, climbing up onto the rock. "She needs you!"

Markus didn't notice that he got wet when a little of the water Sigmund was shaking off dripped on him.

"Huh?"

"You have to write her another letter. As the millionaire."

"But I'm not a millionaire."

"The point is," Sigmund said as he dried himself off, "that Diana Mortensen isn't doing well. She needs someone to confide in. I bet she's just sitting there waiting for you to write. If you tell her who you really are, she'll feel really bad. And it'll be your fault."

"Why do you think that?"

"I just have a feeling. Remember what happened to Marilyn Monroe. You would never forgive yourself, Markus."

"If I don't do what?"

"If you don't write her a letter."

"As the millionaire?"

"Yeah."

"I don't think I can lie to her again, Sigmund. Not to Diana Mortensen."

"I'll help you," Sigmund said calmly. "You don't have a pen and paper with you, do you?"

"Sure," Markus said, "coincidentally."

"Well that's that," Sigmund said. "Not bad, if I do say so myself. Read it out loud."

Marcus began:

> *Dear Diana,*
> *Yes, I feel like I can call you Diana now. Reading your*

letter reinforced my sense that you and I have a connection that extends beyond time and space. The feelings you describe are so familiar to me, because I share them. Reading your letter I felt a deep sense of melancholy, but also of joy—joy at knowing that you're out there. Now it is my humble hope that you will also feel the same joy from my letter. I am harboring a slight hope, Diana, a hope that I can help restore in you a little of the confidence and courage that we all need to go on living and to enjoy the little things in life. Personally, I often find inspiration in nature. A small spring pasqueflower with its white petals tinged with pink and its yellow stamen, a dwarf birch clinging to the barren ground, a glacier in all its frozen splendor, and the sun as it rises over Rondeslottet Peak to start a new day. When I see these sights, I feel alive! Like I am one with nature and kind of like time doesn't exist anymore. Yes, Diana, I often contemplate the nature of time and have concluded that I agree with the poet Gunnar Reiss-Andersen, who put it this way: 'Time is a distance in a bewitched space!' If you know what I mean. Although you are in Hollywood and I am in Norway, we are both in the same space, and the cosmic rays that connect your life to mine know no national borders. I usually put it this way: Enjoy the little things!

I know that you are hunting for the meaning of life, just as I am, but I also know that that is just where you'll find it. A little bird chirping on its branch outside your window, a breath of wind that makes a lock of your hair billow, the trusting gaze of a young admirer. If you get what I mean.

And don't forget, Diana, that no matter how hard it gets,
there will always be a little millionaire sitting somewhere in
the world thinking of you.

In respect, admiration, and sincere friendship,
Markus

It took them two hours to write the letter. The content was
Sigmund's, but most of the wording was Markus's. After all, he
was the expert when it came to writing as someone other than
himself. When they were writing it he thought it was great, but
when he read it out loud he started having doubts. He looked over
at Sigmund a little anxiously.

"Isn't it a little …?"

"A little what?"

"A little too, sort of, grown-up."

"What do you mean by that?"

"That it's so grown-up that it's kind of bordering on childish,
if you know what I mean."

Sigmund didn't know what he meant.

"It's so grown-up because Markus Simonsen is a very grown-
up man. He's … twenty-six."

"Twenty-six?"

"Yeah. You're thirteen, right, and I'm thirteen and a half.
Markus Simonsen the millionaire is you and me put together. So
he's twenty-six. He's as smart as me plus a half and three times
as smart as you."

"Huh?"

"I'm twice as smart as you, right?"

"You are not!"

"But you have more imagination than I do," Sigmund said reassuringly. "Twice as much, as a matter of fact."

Markus was not reassured, but before he could say anything else, Sigmund continued:

"On second thought, I think we ought to add ten more years, since I'm so mature. That makes it thirty-six. Give me the letter."

Markus handed him the letter, and Sigmund crossed out "a little millionaire" and wrote "a thirty-six-year-old millionaire" instead.

"Now I'm done," he said. "I'll take it home and print it out on my dad's computer."

"Hi!"

Ellen Christine had appeared on the stone behind them. She had wet hair and a blue bathing suit. Sigmund stood up.

"I thought you were playing catch with Reidar."

Ellen Christine pushed the wet hair off her forehead. "Ugh, he is so childish. Can I sit here for a bit?"

"Go right ahead," Sigmund said. "We were just leaving. Come on, Markus."

As they walked over to Sigmund's bike, Markus knew that Ellen Christine was still sitting on the rock staring out to sea, not because she wanted to sit there, but because she had said she wanted to, and because she didn't want Sigmund to find out that she was only sitting there because of him.

"Maybe we should go back," he said.

"Why?"

"Well, nah, that's OK," Markus mumbled. "It is true, after all."

"What is?"

"That I have twice as much imagination as you."

CHAPTER 7 Mons's vacation wasn't until the end of July, and they hadn't made any plans yet. That suited Markus just fine, because you never knew what might happen when you were on a trip. If you left the country your passport and money might be stolen, and even here in Norway your car might break down on some highway or other. Sigmund was also going to be home. *The Rich and the Powerful* was at the peak of its success on TV, and Markus and Sigmund had started their own secret fan club for Diana Mortensen. Well, actually it was more of an aid society than a fan club. They called the club HD, which stood for "Help Diana!" The club's headquarters were at the edge of the woods, up above an old stone quarry that people used as an illegal garbage dump and shooting range on the weekends. Neither Markus nor Sigmund had much in the way of carpentry skills, but they had fashioned a shelter out of some boards and an old tarp they had found at the quarry. There they painstakingly compiled a Diana Mortensen archive, which consisted of pictures and clippings from newspapers and magazines. They had pasted a picture of Diana over the one of Norway's Queen Sonja on an empty box of chocolates, and that's where they stored the letter and photograph Diana had sent Markus. They held secret meetings every other day, and there was only ever one item on the agenda: Diana Mortensen.

The more they discussed it, the more concerned they became,

and when they still hadn't received a response to their letter after ten days they started to become genuinely worried.

"I don't like it," Sigmund said. "This silence is unbearable."

"Maybe she could tell that I'm only thirteen," Markus said.

Sigmund looked at him gloomily.

"No thirteen-year-old writes letters like that."

"Maybe she thinks my dad helped me or something."

"If that were the case, I'm sure she would have gotten in touch with your dad."

"Why?"

"Because the letter truly touched her."

"How do you know that?"

"We're not talking about the letter anymore now," Sigmund said. "We're talking about Diana."

"Isn't that what we were doing?"

"You can't run away from reality," Sigmund said gravely.

Markus gave him a puzzled look and asked, "What do you mean by that?"

"You know as well as I do that Diana has problems. There's no use making excuses for her, like she just can't be bothered to write to you or something. If she hasn't written, it's because her problems are even more serious than I had feared."

"Do you think she's been paralyzed?"

"I don't think anything. I just know that it's serious."

Markus nodded.

"Yeah, that's what I figure too."

They had taken an oath up there under the tarp, and the oath was this: "Everything for Diana!"

"What are we going to do?" he asked.

Sigmund looked at his watch, and jumped up saying, "Damn it! I have to go home and eat dinner!"

"Do you think it's drugs?" asked Markus, whose head was still full of Diana Mortensen's problems.

"No," Sigmund said. "I think we're having fish."

"I mean Diana. Do you think she has a drug problem?"

"If she does, it's our job to save her."

"Oh, Sigmund! How can we possibly do that? I mean we're here and she's in Hollywood."

"Yeah," Sigmund said gloomily as they emerged from their lean-to. "That's precisely the problem."

Then he gave Markus a cheerful wave and raced off down the hillside. When he got to the bottom of the quarry, he turned around and shouted:

"I hate fish, but it's good brain food! Maybe it'll help. Everything for Diana!"

"Everything for Diana!" Markus yelled back.

He crawled back under the tarp again and took the photograph out of the old chocolate box. He was on the verge of crying, but didn't.

"You're not the only one who has problems, Diana," he whispered. "Things aren't that easy for me either."

A letter arrived the next day. Markus and Sigmund had agreed that they would open any mail that came from Hollywood together, but Markus couldn't wait. Exactly thirty seconds after he found it in the mailbox, he laid down on his bed and read:

Dear Markus:

I'm sorry it took me so long to answer your letter, but my life is a mess these days. Robert De Niro seems to have fallen in love with me. I don't understand why. I'm just an ordinary Norwegian girl. But I'm not ready to make a commitment. Not yet. At least not to Robert. I don't feel like he's the one. Your letter was charming. Do you know, Markus, I bought myself a little budgie. He's so sweet when he sits on the little perch in his cage and pecks at the bars. I named him Markus. I hope you don't mind. Although he makes me happy, he makes me sad too. Birds really aren't meant to be caged, are they? Actually I really want to set him free, but I don't know if little Markus could make it out there in the craziness of a city this size. Sometimes I feel like I'm a little bird. I dream of getting away from all the cocktail parties, the fake smiles, the envy. Just spread my wings and fly free, way above it all with my little Markus.

By the time he had read this far, Markus was so overwhelmed with emotion that tears were streaming down his cheeks and the letters were swirling around before his eyes. The next few sentences made the whole room swirl.

The reason that I'm writing to you today is that I just found out that my latest movie, The Labyrinth of Love, *is premiering in Norway in August. I've decided to say yes to an invitation to come and do the honors at the premiere. (Imagine that, Markus. Little old me. "Doing the honors!")*

Anyway, I'm going to use the opportunity to take a little vaca-
tion and visit my mom and dad in Horten. Just unwind, be
myself. If you should happen to be in that neck of the woods,
maybe we could meet and have a glass of champagne together.
At any rate, I'll be thinking about you.

Your Diana

"We were supposed to open it together!" Sigmund said when they sat down under the tarp an hour later. He was mad and excited at the same time.

"I couldn't wait."

"We won't talk about that anymore right now," Sigmund said curtly. "We have to prepare."

"For what?"

"For your meeting with Diana. We only have a month."

"Ugh!" Markus said, gulping.

"What do you mean 'ugh'?"

"I … I can't meet Diana Mortensen."

"You have to."

"Why?"

"She needs you."

"She does not!"

"Yes, she does. You have to be able to read between the lines. She's not coming to Norway because of the movie. She's coming because of you."

"Ugh!"

"Would you quit saying 'ugh'?"

"I'll say 'ugh' as much as I want."

"Don't be childish, Wormster."

"Don't call me Wormster!"

"Aren't you the one who's always bragging that you have such a great imagination?"

"I don't brag. You're the one who does that."

"Right. And so which one of us goes glacier hiking with his dad every summer?"

They didn't quarrel often, and when they did Markus usually always backed down first; but this time the fear of meeting Diana Mortensen was greater than the sadness he felt when he argued with Sigmund.

"If I meet Diana Mortensen, I'll faint."

"And if you don't do it, something much worse will happen. Think about Marilyn Monroe!"

"Why should I think about her?"

"She killed herself!"

"You jerk," Markus said and went home. An hour later he called Sigmund. "Meeting," he whispered.

"What?"

"Meeting of the HD club. In half an hour."

"How are we going to prepare?"

He said it quietly, almost in a whisper, but very clearly and without his voice wavering. He knew that if he didn't accept Diana Mortensen's invitation to have a glass of champagne in Horten, he would never forgive himself.

"You have to pretend that you're Markus Simonsen, Junior."

He stared at Sigmund in horror. He wasn't surprised that

Sigmund had a plan, but he was thrown by how hopeless the plan was. Diana didn't want to meet Markus Junior; she wanted to meet Markus Senior. Showing up as a rascally millionaire's son would be a bad, well, a terrible substitute for the actual millionaire who, unfortunately, wasn't real but a ridiculous invention in the head of a thirteen-year-old idiot.

"Markus Simonsen doesn't have a son. He's not married."

"He has a son from a previous marriage. Markus Simonsen, Junior."

Markus noticed that he was sweating. It was starting to get a little challenging to keep track of all the Markus Simonsens that were turning up. There was the real Markus Simonsen: him. Then there was the fake millionaire and mountain climber, Markus Simonsen, and the even faker Markus Simonsen, Junior, who was also him but wasn't him at the same time.

"Why is he called Junior?" he asked hoarsely.

"Millionaires' sons are always named Junior."

"But I'm not a millionaire's son."

"No. You have to pretend you are."

"She doesn't want to meet the junior. She wants to meet the senior."

"Yeah, but the junior is the spitting image of his father. He'll meet Diana and restore her faith in humanity, just like the senior would have done."

Markus laughed hollowly. It was easy for Sigmund. He could just sit there and use his super-brain to make plans. He didn't need to pretend he was junior anybody. And come to think of it, why didn't he have to do it? He was older than Markus and much better at speaking than Markus was. It was a brilliant idea! He suggested it. Sigmund's face got pale, but his voice was scornful when he said:

"What, are you chicken?"

"Yes," said Markus, which was the truth.

"You were the one who wrote the first letter. You're responsible for all this."

"Not for the junior idea. You're the one who came up with that. Junior is your responsibility."

Sigmund stopped and looked at Markus for a second.

"We'll flip a coin. Heads you win, tails I win."

Before Markus could say anything, Sigmund took a coin out of his pocket and tossed it up in the air. It was heads.

"I won," Markus said, relieved. "So you'll meet Diana."

"What do you mean?"

"You lost the coin toss!"

"Do you mean that meeting Diana Mortensen is losing? Like a punishment?"

"No, but …"

"Is that how you see her? Like suddenly she's some kind of a leper or something?"

"I didn't mean …"

"If you think she's so awful, I don't get why you wrote to her in the first place. *Losing!* Getting to meet someone that half of Norway can only dream of catching a glimpse of. I would have considered that an honor!"

"Then you go meet her instead."

"Nope," Sigmund said calmly. "I lost the coin toss. You won, you lucky dog!"

Markus knew there was no point discussing it. No matter what he said, Sigmund would twist his words until he got what he wanted, and it was obvious that he wanted Markus to meet Diana. He gave up.

"Where are you going to be when I meet her?" he asked forlornly.

"I'll be nearby. Just relax."

"I never relax," Markus mumbled, "and I have no idea how a millionaire's son would act."

Sigmund smiled at him and said, "But I do."

Markus sighed. "Yeah, I figured."

It was starting to get dark by the time they'd made a list of everything Markus had to learn to convince Diana Mortensen that he really was the son of a millionaire: He had to memorize the rules of golf and tennis, acquire a basic knowledge of how to speculate on the stock market, familiarize himself with the world of foreign currency exchange, get used to wearing a suit and tie every day, learn the rules of etiquette by heart, practice engaging in polite conversation, and, last but not least, learn how to behave normally in a fancy restaurant. In other words, he pretty much had to spend his summer vacation doing stuff he didn't want to do.

"Do I have to?" he moaned.

"Everything for Diana!" Sigmund said, patting him on the shoulder.

"Right, of course. Everything for Diana. When do I start my training?"

"Tomorrow. Now we're going to write Diana a letter."

"And tell her I want to meet her?"

"No, I think that had better be a surprise. We'll write that you have a son."

"I don't have a son."

"That the millionaire has a son."

"Oh, right," Markus said. "Maybe the son will break his leg this summer."

Dear Diana:

Thank you for your letter. Such wonderful news that you're coming to Norway this August. I would like nothing better than to meet you. Maybe we could go for a hike in the mountains or play a game of golf if I'm able to get out of an important meeting I have scheduled then. My son is also eager to meet you. Ah, I don't think I've mentioned that I have a son. From a previous marriage. He's a chip off the old block. My little curly-haired youngster is as curious as a squirrel and as clever as a mink. But at the same time he's a thoughtful lad. There's not a thing in the world I can't talk to Markus Junior about. At the moment he's reading Shakespeare. He's a bit of an actor, actually. I wouldn't be surprised if he went on to play Romeo in Romeo and Juliet *one of these days. He's a joy and a comfort to his father when the going gets rough. Yes, dear Diana. That's a bit about my son. I was both proud and pleased that you named your budgie Markus. That makes me feel even closer to you than before. Maybe I should get a bird too. A little Diana that can*

wake my son and me up with its merry twittering on light
summer mornings.

I hope to hear from you again.

Your Markus

Markus was the one who had come up with the part about the little curly-haired youngster who was as curious as a squirrel and as clever as a mink, but when he read the letter aloud to Sigmund he had second thoughts.

"Maybe I should get rid of that part about the curly hair?"

Sigmund shook his head.

"Why? 'Curly-haired youngster' is brilliant."

"But I don't have curly hair."

"No, not now. But when you meet Diana you will."

"That's what I was afraid of," Markus said, sealing the envelope.

CHAPTER 8 "How much does a tennis ball weigh?"

"It must weigh more than two ounces but less than two and one-sixteenth ounces."

Sigmund nodded.

"How long is it?"

"A tennis ball doesn't have a length," Markus said. "It's round."

Sigmund had reserved a tennis court at the recreation center for eleven a.m. Now it was ten fifteen and they were sitting in the center's cafeteria memorizing the rules. Sigmund was wearing white shorts, a white T-shirt, and a headband. Markus was wearing brown corduroy shorts and a light-blue T-shirt. They had rented rackets from the center. Neither of them had ever played tennis before, but Sigmund had brought along a book called *Improve Your Tennis*.

"I mean, what is the diameter of a tennis ball?"

"I don't understand why I have to know that!"

"A tennis ball must be between two and a half inches and two and five-eighths inches in diameter."

"There's no way she's going to ask me what the diameter of a tennis ball is. Or how much one weighs, either."

"You can't know that."

"There isn't anyone in the whole world who cares what a tennis ball weighs."

"Yes there is. Stefan Edberg, for example."

"Who's Stefan Edberg?"

"A tennis player."

"Diana Mortensen isn't a tennis player."

"Really? What do you think movie stars do in their free time?"

"They … they relax, I guess."

"Exactly. By playing tennis. What about the racket?"

"What about it?"

"What's it supposed to look like?"

"I don't care!" Markus said.

Sigmund nodded again.

"It's perfectly acceptable not to care. There aren't actually any rules for what size or shape a tennis racket has to have."

"That's ridiculous," Markus said grumpily.

"What is?"

"That a tennis ball can't be longer than …"

"Two and five-eighths inches."

"Yeah, but the racket could be several miles long. Then I could just make myself a racket that's bigger than the whole tennis court and then I could be world champion."

"That's enough about the racket," Sigmund said. "Now let's talk about 'The Code of Tennis, or The Unofficial Rules of Good Tennis Sportsmanship.'"

For the next forty minutes they reviewed not only "The Code of Tennis, or The Unofficial Rules of Good Tennis Sportsmanship," but also the official rules of the game, how to calculate points, how to grip the racket, how to serve the ball, and useful strokes like forehand drive, backhand drive, smash, and volley.

Markus felt like his head was full of hundreds of tennis balls that weighed at least two ounces and that were whooshing around in there every which way. He was pretty confused, but it seemed like Sigmund was in full control.

"Now you've mastered the basic theory," he said as they entered the rec center.

"I have?"

"Yes. Now you just have to learn to play."

"Do *you* know how to play?"

"No, but I've seen people do it on TV. It doesn't look that hard."

It was hard. Neither of them had a particularly well-developed feel for the ball. The few times they happened to make contact with the ball, it flew straight into the net or up toward the ceiling. Except for when it disappeared over the netting that separated the two courts located in the large indoor facility from each other. If Markus was the world's worst tennis player, and there were a lot of indications that this might be the case, then Sigmund was the second worst, but he wouldn't admit it. Every time he missed, he would make an excuse for why. He would even pretend he'd done it on purpose.

"Now why do you think I just hit the ball up toward the ceiling?"

"Because you weren't able to hit it over the net?"

"No, to show you how not to hit it. Did you notice how I was holding the racket crooked?"

"Yes."

"You shouldn't hold it that way."

"Of course not. I know that."

"And my stroke proved it."

Somehow or other, Markus managed to fumble the ball over the net. Sigmund hit it, and it flew over the netting into the court next to them.

"I did it again. Do you see?"

"I saw a long time ago," Markus mumbled, going over to get the ball.

Ellen Christine came into the room along with Mona. She was showing up everywhere these days, Markus thought. Both girls had tan legs and short, white skirts. Markus had brown shorts and short, white legs. People sure do vary.

"Hi, Wormster," Mona said. "I didn't know you played tennis."

Markus tried to say something, but it just came out as a sort of snort. Ellen Christine had walked over to the netting, and he could tell from her back that she was smiling at Sigmund.

"Hi, Sigmund! Are you here?"

"No," Sigmund said. "I'm in London."

"Do you guys … do you guys want to play doubles?"

"No, we like being single," Sigmund replied tersely.

Ellen Christine turned around and walked back over to Mona again.

"I think she's stalking me," Sigmund said when Markus came back with the ball. "She probably called and found out that I was here. She calls all the time."

Markus nodded.

"She's definitely in love with you."

"Yeah, but she has about as much chance as a raindrop in the desert. Now why don't we practice our serves."

Sigmund had said "we," but he meant Markus. He put down his racket and started picking up the balls Markus had tried to hit over the net. There was no point asking why he didn't try hitting them back instead. That would just lead to another pointless discussion. Besides, it didn't take much imagination to understand that it was because Sigmund didn't want Ellen Christine to figure out that Markus wasn't the only one who was a terrible tennis player. Markus served and served, to the east and the west, to the north and the south. Every once in a while he heard a faint giggle from the other court, but he clenched his teeth together and bravely swung his desperate, hopeless strokes until it was finally twelve o'clock and their hour was up.

"It was going a little better at the end there," Markus said, picking up a ball that had gotten stuck in the net.

"Really, was it?" Sigmund said absentmindedly, stealing a glance over at the other court.

"Hello, girls!"

Ellen Christine appeared over by the netting in a flash.

"Yes?"

"Do you want to go out with us and have dinner?"

Markus couldn't believe his ears.

"Ugh," he whispered, but he was the only one who heard it.

Ellen Christine was beaming. She looked as if she'd won the lottery.

"Dinner? Where? At your house?"

"No, at L'Étoile."

"Ugh," Markus said again. A little louder, but still nobody heard him.

L'Étoile was a restaurant downtown that had a dance floor. It was extremely fancy and very expensive.

Markus lost hold of the tennis ball. It rolled slowly over toward Sigmund, who picked it up and started tossing it nonchalantly from one hand to the other. Mona had also come over to the netting, and the girls started whispering to each other. Ellen Christine was a little red in the face, and Mona was looking at Sigmund in suspicion.

"Do you *mean* it?"

"If you don't want to go, we'll just ask someone else. It doesn't matter to us."

He turned toward Markus, who was walking over to him. Extremely slowly.

"Isn't that right, Markus?"

"Yarglf," Markus coughed. He had a lump in his throat. A huge one.

Ellen Christine tried to act calm.

"Sure we could. When were you thinking?"

"Next Saturday," Sigmund said. "Six o'clock."

Markus was trying desperately to say something as Sigmund pushed him out of the building. The lump was still in his throat, and he was coughing like crazy. As they entered the locker room, he heard the sound of a girl squealing in delight.

"You are completely insane," he groaned. "I don't want to go out to eat with Ellen Christine."

"I'm the one who's going with her. You're going with Mona."

"I'm not *going* with Mona."

"Relax. It's just for one night."

"I have no idea how to behave in a restaurant."

"No, precisely. That's why we have to go."

"Couldn't we go out to dinner, just the two of us?"

"It wouldn't be the same."

Markus desperately searched for a way to get out of it.

"I don't have any money. L'Étoile has got to be the most expensive restaurant in town."

"I have money," Sigmund said, giving Markus a friendly smile. "I've been saving up for a computer."

He winked at Markus and stepped into the shower.

"You shouldn't spend the money you've been saving on a restaurant!" Markus shouted, knowing what Sigmund was going to say before he even said it:

"Everything for Diana!"

"You're asking if we have any books about manners and etiquette?" the librarian asked, looking at the two boys standing on the other side of the counter with interest.

"Yes," Sigmund replied. "We'd like to learn a little about good manners."

The librarian was an older woman who had been working at the local library for over forty years. She had only six months to go before she retired. She loved children, but was not always impressed by their reading habits.

"You're sure you don't want something with a little more speed and excitement?" she asked warily.

"Good manners can be quite exciting," Sigmund said in all seriousness.

Markus gulped and nodded as if to say that Sigmund couldn't be more right.

The librarian was in ecstasy.

"Indeed, you're quite right about that, my boy. But there are so few young people these days who understand that."

"Hmm," said Sigmund, "we're rather unusual."

"Yes, so I'm starting to gather," the librarian said enthusiastically.

"Let's see … Of course we have the old edition from 1960. But it's as thick as the Bible."

"Ah, yes, the etiquette bible," Sigmund said. "I know that one."

The librarian eyed him suspiciously for a second. It wasn't always so easy to tell if Sigmund was kidding or not.

"Do you mean that you've read it?"

"I've browsed through it," Sigmund said breezily. "Don't you have anything more up to date?"

"Yeeeaaah, of course we have *The Guide to Good Manners in the '90s*. It's only 190 pages long."

"That's perfect. We'd like to borrow two copies, please."

"Two?"

"Yes. We're planning to use them for our club."

Markus was flabbergasted. Surely Sigmund wasn't planning on revealing the club to the librarian? He poked his index finger hard into Sigmund's back, but he needn't have. Sigmund had realized that he was about to let the cat out of the bag.

"I mean … um … our etiquette club!"

Now the librarian really was impressed. She found two copies of the book and offered to help them if they needed any more literature on the subject.

After Sigmund had thanked her for her offer and Markus had tripped over the shoelaces he'd forgotten to tie, they exited the library, leaving behind them a librarian who had gained a whole new level of respect for today's youth.

Markus lay in bed reading. He had gotten to page 9: "Meeting and Greeting":

"Being able to market yourself is more important today than it has ever been before. First impressions are often critical: It is important to appear happy and charming as well as to imprint your name so that others remember it, either with the help of a business card or by stating your name loudly and clearly …"

He set the book down on his comforter. There was a lot to learn here. If there was one thing he had failed to do so far in life, it was market himself. His first impression was usually just so-so. He tried to remember the last time he'd appeared happy and charming, but couldn't think of a single time. And when had he ever imprinted his name? Never. He had simply resigned himself to his nickname Wormster, unhappily and without much charm, without presenting the people who called him that with so much as a paltry business card. That pretty much explained it. Maybe that's why they teased him. Because he was so incredibly unhappy. He'd never seen a happy person being teased. He used to think that was why they were so happy, but now he saw that it was the other way around. They weren't happy because they weren't being teased. They weren't being teased because they were happy. He had been the victim of a terrible misunderstanding, without even suspecting that the answer to all his problems had been just around the corner this whole time. At the Ruud Public Library. This little book was nothing less than a user's manual for how to have a happy life. He read on in feverish excitement:

"In many cultures cheek kissing is a ritual or social gesture used to indicate friendship, perform a greeting, offer congratulations, comfort someone, or show respect. It does not necessarily indicate sexual or romantic interest. What rules govern cheek kissing? Do you kiss someone on the right or the left cheek and, if both, which one do you kiss first? Should your lips actually touch the other person's cheek or not? Are the rules the same in Norway as in other countries?"

This was tremendously interesting. When he met Diana he would make a huge fool of himself if he didn't even know which cheek to kiss her on. Because according to the etiquette guide he was going to have to kiss her; there was unfortunately no doubt about that. Flash a charming smile, imprint the name Markus Simonsen, Junior, and give her a kiss on the cheek—that was the very least she would expect from him. This book had all the answers. He read on:

"It is difficult to accomplish this elegantly. Observe how the members of the royal family do it—they kiss first the right cheek then the left. You must always first turn your right cheek to the other person's right cheek and then your left to their left. It is very difficult to carry this off flawlessly."

Yeah, you could say that again! It was just like dancing. It was totally impossible to do the right steps when he was trying to think about what they were. He had learned this bitter lesson at the dance class his mom had sent him to when he was seven. If he was thinking one step to the right and two to the left, it turned out it was supposed to be the other way around. He had shuffled around like a preoccupied zombie while the others, who weren't thinking at all, floated rhythmically across the dance floor. "Don't think so much, Markus," the dance teacher had said. "You just have to move naturally with the music." But moving naturally would take a lot of practice. He was starting to think that Sigmund's plan to go out to a restaurant with Ellen Christine and Mona wasn't so dumb after all. It would give him the opportunity to practice some of this stuff.

With these thoughts he drifted off to sleep, where he met Diana Mortensen naturally and charmingly. He was just about to give her a kiss—which cheek was it again?—when his father's yell woke him up.

"Help!"

He was walking in his sleep again. He was leaning over his father with a charming smile plastered on his face.

"Oh, Markus, is that you? I thought it was ... oh my God, Markus! I was having such a terrible dream ... and then when I woke up ... I thought you were ... a murderer ... Were you walking in your sleep?"

Mons rubbed his eyes and both of them started coming to.

"Yeah," Markus said. "I was dreaming too."

"What about? Your smile was so creepy."

"I was dreaming I was charming," Markus said.

CHAPTER 9 "Do you have to wear gloves to be properly dressed nowadays, Dad?"

Markus was standing in front of the mirror in the hallway looking at his face. He'd slicked his hair down with water and parted it on one side. Mons emerged from the living room, eyeing his son uneasily. He didn't understand what was happening. Markus was growing up at a furious pace these days, that much was clear. In just four days he'd become much more polite than he had been before. He was opening the door for Mons when he left for work, constantly pointing out that his name was Markus, which of course his dad already knew, and incessantly smiling that same charming smile he'd worn when he was sleepwalking. It seemed like he was turning into an old man in a thirteen-year-old's body, and Mons wasn't sure he liked that. If Markus weren't his own son, he'd say the boy was turning into a little sycophant.

"Search me," he said a little nervously. "I've never really thought about it."

"But I have," Markus said. "You don't necessarily have to wear gloves to be properly dressed."

"Well, that's a relief," his father said.

"Gloves are optional—only if you want an attractive accessory to go with your formal spring attire. Otherwise you don't need a hat or gloves these days, if it's not too cold out. But, Dad, what do we do if we absolutely don't want our guests to wear jeans?"

"Now there's a problem I haven't given much thought to," Mons said, glancing down at his watch.

Markus nodded.

"I rather expect there aren't many who have. But sometimes we want people to dress up a little without necessarily having to wear a tuxedo or tails, right?"

"We certainly do."

Markus opened the front door and flashed his dad a charming smile.

"Have a good day, Dad."

Mons sighed heavily and slowly walked away down the street with his head bowed.

Markus stood in the doorway and watched him. He had a lump in his throat. He might be acting like a gentleman, but he felt like an idiot. Every time he bowed politely to his dad, he wanted to fling himself around Mons's neck instead, but he couldn't do that. He had to practice being on his best behavior until it was completely natural, and he could walk through life with his head held high. So far it was awful walking with his head held high. It felt like several tons of fear and anxiety were pushing his head down. If he'd had a choice, he would have devoted more time to learning how to have good manners. Seventy or eighty years, for example. But he didn't have a choice. He was going to L'Étoile tomorrow, and Diana Mortensen was going to be in Horten in two weeks. They hadn't gotten a response to their last letter yet. Maybe she'd changed her mind or gotten a major role in something, meaning she had to stay in Hollywood after all. Then he could relax a little about the politeness. Try to enjoy his childhood for as long as he could. Well, maybe "enjoy" wasn't the right word, but at any rate it was better than the whole trying-to-have-good-manners business. He'd read the book four times and discussed every single chapter with Sigmund up at headquarters. It seemed so simple on paper, but in reality it was much worse. Just like dance class. Maybe it wasn't necessary for everyone to dance their way through life or market themselves all the time. He didn't know. He only knew that if there was anyone who definitely needed to learn how to market himself, and do it awfully soon, it was him.

He shut the door and stared at himself in the mirror again. His slicked-down hair lay on top of his scalp like a layer of fresh asphalt. He looked like a gangster. No, there was just no way out of it. It would have to be curls. He was looking forward to that the way a criminal looks forward to a life sentence.

Then the doorbell rang. He messed up his hair as best he could and opened the door. It was Sigmund, who said, "Hi. I rented tuxedos."

"Is that necessary?" Markus asked. "Can't we wear suits instead?"

"No, we have to keep up appearances, you know. Did any letters come today?"

"No."

"I'm sure it'll come," Sigmund said cheerfully. "Put on your tuxedo."

"Can't I wait until tomorrow?"

"We have to see if it fits, don't we?"

Markus felt a little glimmer of hope.

"Yeah, maybe it won't fit. Then ..."

"Then we'll exchange it for one that does."

"Oh, right."

The tuxedo fit him to a T. Markus looked at himself in the mirror and was almost impressed by the young man staring back at him. The tuxedo was black with a red cummerbund, red bow tie, and a red pocket handkerchief that Sigmund had folded perfectly and pushed down into the one breast pocket. No one would be able to tell that the cuff links weren't made of real gold.

"Elegant," Sigmund said.

Markus nodded.

"Can I take it off now?"

"No, I think you should wear it today so you get used to it. And then there's your hair."

"What about my hair?" Markus asked, although he already knew what was coming.

"We have to curl it."

"Can't I wait until I meet Diana?"

"No, you can't," Sigmund said decidedly. "Tomorrow's dinner is the dress rehearsal, and at the dress rehearsal everyone wears full makeup and costume, just like at the premiere."

"I refuse to wear makeup!" Markus yelped.

There were limits. True he'd promised to do everything for Diana, but "everything" meant everything except makeup!

"Relax," Sigmund said. "In a way curling your hair is the same as wearing makeup. I brought my sister's curling iron."

Five hours later, Markus was walking back and forth across the living room floor with his head bowed, his hair freshly curled, and wearing a tuxedo, while Sigmund bombarded him with questions about how to behave in a restaurant.

"Who leads the way to the table, the gentleman or the lady?"

"If you reserved a table and the maître d' shows you to your table, the guest, I mean the woman, follows him to the table and the man, or the person acting as host, goes last," Markus said mechanically.

"And if a couple is walking in together to look for a table on their own?"

"Then the man goes first."

"Right. Who sits where, if you end up in a restaurant where there's a table with a built-in bench on one side and a chair on the other side?"

"Then you should find a different restaurant."

"I'm being serious, Markus!"

"Then the woman should get to sit on the bench, with a view out at the room. How about a game of Yahtzee?"

"No. We've invited guests to a restaurant. What can we expect from the maître d' and the headwaiter?"

Markus sighed heavily and answered as best he could. When they had finished going through the restaurant rules once, they started at the beginning again. By four-thirty in the afternoon, Markus knew the whole chapter by heart. The maître d' and the headwaiter at L'Étoile were going to have their hands full. Mons already did. At quarter to five, they heard him open the front door.

"Hurry," Sigmund said. "Slip out to the kitchen and get a glass of water."

"Why?"

"To be polite. I'm sure he's thirsty after a long day at the office."

Markus went to the kitchen while Sigmund stayed in the living room to welcome Mons home.

"Oh hi, Sigmund. I didn't know you were here."

"Good day, Mr. Simonsen. Have you had a tiring day at the office?"

"Only so-so. Where's Markus? I brought him a little start-of-summer present."

Mons pulled a soccer ball out of a plastic bag and showed it to Sigmund. At the same instant, Markus walked into the room from the kitchen with a tray bearing a single wineglass, half full of water.

"Would you care for a glass of water, Dad?"

Mons turned around. Markus put on his most charming smile. "Whaaaaaaaat!?!"

His dad howled like a cat in a tree, took a step backward, tripped and landed in an armchair, and lay there on his back while groaning loudly. The soccer ball rolled across the floor and disappeared somewhere under the TV.

"Or maybe you aren't thirsty?" Markus said meekly.

"You ... you ... you look like ... Little Lord Fauntleroy!" Mons whispered hoarsely.

"Yeah, he does, doesn't he, Mr. Simonsen," Sigmund said with satisfaction. "He's rather stylish."

Mons Simonsen was a peace-loving man with a relaxed view of child rearing. As long as Markus came home by the agreed time and didn't snatch purses away from old ladies, he could pretty much do whatever he wanted. If he'd greeted his dad with green hair and rings in his ears and nose, Mons would probably have been a little taken aback, but certainly wouldn't have demanded that he dye his hair back to normal and take off the jewelry. It's even possible that he would have worn a small ring in his own ear as an expression of solidarity with his son. Just around the house, of course. Wearing an earring at work was out of the question. But those damn curls pushed him over the edge. It had been so long since Mons had exploded that he'd almost forgotten how to do it, and for that very reason his fury was extra-intense.

He managed to stand up while staring at Markus with his mouth agape, snorting like a bull preparing to attack a matador. Then he started to growl.

Markus, who was still trying to smile even though he sensed catastrophe looming, asked, "Um, do you like my hairdo, Dad?"

Then Mons exploded.

"You look like a ... You look like a ... snobblesnoot!" he screamed.

"Um, what do you mean by snobblesnoot, Mr. Simonsen?" Sigmund asked, interested.

"And not a word from you, Mr. ... Mr. Meddlehead!" Mons roared.

Mr. Meddlehead kept his mouth shut. Markus wasn't smiling anymore. He was standing completely still while his father hopped up and down, flailing his arms around and screaming words at

Markus that were completely new to both of them, but that Mons had resorted to because he couldn't find the right words to express the fury that filled him.

"You look like a ... penguifer!" he roared. "A shevelwit! A muff-o'-shanter! Smooth out that darned wig, you curly-haired ... wormwig!"

"Don't call me wormwig, Dad," Markus said softly. "Please. That's what they call me at school."

"What?"

"Well, they call me Wormster."

All Mons's fury evaporated instantly. He stood there with his arms hanging, staring at Markus.

"Markus ... I ... I had no idea ... I ..."

He took a step toward Markus and reached out with his arms helplessly. It was both an attempt to show that he was sorry and a plea for his son to fling himself into his arms. Markus took a step back toward the kitchen door.

"*I* thought you would think I was handsome."

"You *are* handsome, Markus. You are ... very handsome. I just ..."

"Why did you call me wormwig?"

"I didn't mean it ... You're not a wormwig. You're probably not wearing a wig at all. I'm the wormwig. Do you ... do you two want some ice cream? I bought ... strawberry."

Markus didn't respond. He had turned his back on his father and headed for his room. Sigmund and Mons heard him lock the door from inside.

Sigmund stood up.

"Well, I ought to be getting home."

Mons didn't respond. Sigmund turned around in the doorway and said encouragingly:

"It's just the generation gap, Mr. Simonsen. Don't take it so hard. It happens all the time."

Mons stood there in the middle of the floor for a little while after Sigmund left. He took the container of strawberry ice cream out of a paper bag, walked to the kitchen, and set it on the counter. He went back to the living room, where he sat on the sofa and stared at a photograph hanging on the wall. He had taken it himself, ten years ago, when his wife was sitting in a recliner with Markus in her lap. She was smiling and Markus was laughing. When she died, he had asked if they should take it down from the wall, but Markus had said no. Mons smiled fleetingly at the photograph. Then he put his head in his hands and cried. When he was done crying he went out into the kitchen to make coffee. He wished he could erase the last half hour of his life and eat strawberry ice cream with Markus.

What he didn't know was that Markus was sitting in his room feeling just as bad as he was. He knew without a doubt that Mons hadn't meant to call him a wormwig, but had only done it because it had been such a big shock for him to see Markus in a black tuxedo with curly hair. He know full well that his dad's distress was much more genuine than his fury. He wanted to open the door, rush into the living room, and tell him he didn't have to feel bad and that he would never curl his hair again for the rest of his life. But he couldn't do it. He just couldn't make himself do it. It was some kind of idiotic stubbornness or cowardice. Yeah, *that* was really cowardly. It wouldn't take more than a single word or a smile. No, not a smile. At least not a charming one. This didn't have anything at all to do with being charming. It had to do with longing. Suddenly they were so far away from each other, and he longed to be close to his dad so dreadfully.

Why don't I do it? he thought. All I have to do is just do it!

And so he did.

He rushed to the door, unlocked it, and ran into the living room. His father was sitting with a coffee cup in front of him. He looked very alone. When Markus entered the room, he stood up, took a step toward him, then stopped and ran his fingers through his hair. Markus stopped too. They stood there looking at each other. One was thirty-nine with thinning hair and wearing a gray suit and a blue-striped shirt. The other was thirteen with curly hair and wearing a tuxedo and cummerbund. Neither of them knew who took the first step, but suddenly they were holding each other and squeezing so that their hearts almost burst.

"I miss Mom," Markus gasped. "Oh, Dad, Dad, I miss her so much!"

His dad stroked his curly hair.

"My little boy," he whispered. "My boy, my boy, my boy."

They stood that way until everything that could be good again was good again, and the things that were terrible were a little less terrible.

Markus took the red handkerchief out of his breast pocket and blew his nose.

"You shouldn't get your fancy handkerchief dirty," Mons whispered.

Markus smiled. His own smile.

"Actually, I should. It is a handkerchief, after all."

Mons smiled back.

"Is there anything you want to do?"

"Yeah. I want to eat strawberry ice cream."

"Oh no! The ice cream! I'm sure it's melted!"

"That doesn't matter," Markus said cheerfully. "Melted strawberry ice cream is also good."

He lay in the bathtub and repeated to himself:

"Take your seats quietly and go through the menu with the headwaiter. Then you can discuss wines, prices, wine-food pairings, et cetera. In some establishments you may be able to sit in a private room while you plan the meal …"

Markus gulped. Were they going to sit in a private room at L'Étoile? He hoped not. For some reason or other, the idea of sitting in a private room was even more frightening than the idea of sitting in a room packed with hundreds of other diners. That would be unsettling enough of course, but a private room with Sigmund, Mona, and Ellen Christine was even worse. He had the feeling he was sweating even though his body was immersed in water, as Sigmund sometimes said.

"What is the right way to eat a salad?"

"Markus, did you drown?"

"No, Dad. I'm just lying here relaxing."

He'd been lying in the tub for half an hour, and the water was starting to cool down. That didn't matter because he was rather warm. He could have lain there all day, no problem. But he had plenty of problems. He read on:

"The proper way to eat is either using just a fork or both a fork and knife, but if you're going to be picky, it is not considered correct to slice your lettuce."

He wasn't planning on being picky, but he definitely had a feeling that Sigmund would be.

"Markus! You have to finish up now!"

He sighed and raised his body up out of the water. Then he put on the tracksuit that was lying on the bathroom floor. He had made plans to take a short morning jog with Sigmund. Markus seldom went jogging, but Sigmund said it would help him relax. He had some serious doubts, but ultimately Sigmund was calling the shots.

When he walked into the kitchen, Mons looked at him in astonishment.

"What happened to your … handsome curls?"

"They're lying in the bathtub."

"What did you say?"

"I washed my hair."

Mons looked like he was feeling guilty again.

"But, Markus … You didn't have to do that. I was just starting to get used to them."

"I wasn't," Markus responded, putting on his sneakers.

"Where are you going?"

"Jogging."

"Well, that'll put hair on your chest," Mons said cheerfully.

Markus rolled his eyes and said, "Next time you buy me a tracksuit, I want a different color."

"What color would you like?"

"Camouflage," Markus said, walking out the door with his

head bowed. Dad shouldn't think that everything was all right just because they'd eaten strawberry ice cream together.

Markus and Sigmund jogged slowly up the path toward the stone quarry. They went up to their headquarters and crawled in under the tarp.

"Why did you get rid of your curls?"

Markus had been expecting that question. Sigmund had been unhappy and not very charming the whole time they'd been jogging. Every now and then he had looked over at Markus out of the corner of his eye and shaken his head, as if he'd seen something he didn't like.

"Turns out I washed them out."

"Turns out?"

"Yeah. Coincidentally."

"People don't coincidentally wash their curls out."

"I thought they would stay in."

"We can't make new ones either. My sister is out of town. She took her curling iron with her."

"That's too bad."

Markus tried to look sad. Sigmund looked at him gloomily.

"We'll part it in the middle instead."

"No! Not parted down the middle! I refuse! I'm going to look like a gangster!"

"No you won't. You're going to look great. Not as great as you would with curls, of course, but very presentable."

After a few pointless objections, Markus gave up. Parting his hair in the middle passed by a vote of one-to-one. After a brief planning session for their restaurant visit later that night, and repeated assurances from Markus that he would chill out, they ended the meeting with their two voices cheering "Help Diana!" in unison.

When they emerged from the hut, there was a man standing down in the stone quarry. He was holding a rifle and aiming at some tin cans that were stacked up right below them.

"Hey!" Sigmund yelled. "Don't shoot!"

Markus grabbed Sigmund's arm and said, "Shhh. Don't say anything. Maybe he'll hit me."

"Very nice, Markus," Mons said slightly nervously. "Parting your hair in the middle suits you."

When Markus had explained that he was going out to dinner with Sigmund and two girls, his father had been really surprised, but also relieved. That explained his son's recent behavior. The boy had fallen in love for the first time, and now he wanted to make an impression on the young lady. Thirteen was young. Mons himself hadn't fallen in love for the first time until he was fourteen years old. Then he'd asked the girl next door to the movies, but hadn't had the courage to actually show up. He had thought Markus was just as shy as he had been, but it appeared he'd been thoroughly wrong about that. His son was obviously turning into a sophisticated little man of the world. That was nice, but also a little sad. Mons thought the tuxedo and the hair part were a little bit much, but on the other hand he wasn't really up on the latest fashion trends. When he was young bellbottoms and Beatles hairdos were in. So now it was tuxedos and parting your hair in the middle. Times change. He'd given Markus twenty dollars, which he'd thought would be enough for hamburgers and a soda at the snack bar. It never occurred to him that they would dine at L'Étoile, and it didn't occur to Markus to mention that either. You had to maintain some degree of mystery, especially with the people you were closest to.

"I'll comb it out tomorrow, Dad."

"Do whatever you want, son. As long as you have a good time."

Markus nodded gloomily.

"Bye, Dad."

"Bye … Oh, wait a sec!"

Mons ran into the living room and got the red handkerchief Markus had blown his nose on the night before.

"You forgot this."

The handkerchief was freshly washed and ironed. Mons tried to spread it out neatly. He didn't succeed.

"I'll do it, Dad."

In a couple of simple movements, Markus artfully folded the handkerchief and put it in his breast pocket. Mons gazed at him, impressed.

"If you have to blow your nose then …"

"I'll do it as quietly as possible, with my head turned away from the others. I know all about it, Dad."

"But I don't," Mons mumbled as the door shut behind Markus, who was on his way to his grand dress rehearsal in formal restaurant etiquette.

CHAPTER 10 Ellen Christine and Mona were already standing there waiting when Markus and Sigmund's taxi pulled up in front of L'Étoile. That was mistake number one. Never make a woman wait.

"Is it a wedding?" the cabdriver asked as Sigmund handed him a ten.

"No, it's just a small, private gathering."

The driver glanced at Markus out of the corner of his eye and grinned. "The Norwegian mafia, huh? Heh, heh."

"Heh, heh," Markus laughed ominously, getting out of the cab.

Sigmund had put on a white tuxedo jacket with black pants, a black bow tie and black cummerbund. Both he and Markus had white silk scarves around their necks. Sigmund wore the tuxedo as if he'd been born in it. He kept his hair the way it usually was, but then it wasn't his dress rehearsal. He was the director and had brought along a pad and paper to jot down any potential blunders the lead actor might make. He's going to be using that a lot, Markus thought as he tried to smile charmingly at the girls. He was sure they would burst out laughing when they saw him, but they didn't. They stared at him with their mouths agape.

"Good evening, ladies," Sigmund said, bowing chivalrously.

"Where's Markus?" Ellen Christine asked.

"Right here," Markus said pathetically.

"You look so … grown-up," Mona said, without any hint of sarcasm in her voice.

"So stylish," Ellen Christine said. "I didn't recognize you."

"Variety is the spice of life," Markus mumbled. Suddenly he felt a lot better, but he still wasn't quite sure if this was some kind of calm before the storm, or before everyone burst out laughing.

"You don't look so bad yourselves," he added cautiously and was quite surprised when both girls blushed. That was something completely foreign. Usually he was the one blushing when girls talked to *him*. It sank in that they really thought he looked good. Well, well, there's no accounting for taste, and that's a good thing. He felt like he was really starting to get into the swing of things.

"You can make a plain dress more formal by accessorizing with just the right little handbag and an elegant pair of shoes," he recited from memory.

"I got them for my birthday," Mona whispered, glancing down at her silver-colored shoes.

"And did a photograph of the celebrant appear in the newspaper?" Markus inquired politely.

"Huh?"

"One presumes that if a festive occasion is mentioned in the paper, people will interpret this as a sign that you will be receiving callers."

Sigmund was starting to get a little uncomfortable next to him, but Markus didn't notice. He was really getting up to speed now.

"This may result in many forgotten acquaintances, such as old classmates, getting in touch with you to extend their birthday greetings."

"Why don't we head in now?" Sigmund suggested.

"That is one of the most delightful aspects of birthdays," Markus said in a loud, clear voice, holding the door open for the girls.

As Mona passed him, he winked at her playfully. She jumped nervously and scurried into the restaurant.

"There's no need to overdo it," Sigmund whispered as they checked their silk scarves in the cloakroom, but Markus was really into his sophisticated man-of-the-world role. There was no way out of it. He just had to keep going.

"My name is Markus," he told the cloakroom attendant.

"Oh, it is, is it?"

"Yes. I'd really like to imprint it. Markus!"

The cloakroom attendant contemplated him carefully. Slowly he said, "I will never forget it."

"No," Markus said calmly, "I figure you won't."

The girls had gone to the bathroom. Sigmund had sat down on a chair to wait. Markus kept chatting with the cloakroom attendant.

"Do you have a special room where we can sit and plan our meal?"

"No. We don't have one of those," the cloakroom attendant said a little crossly. Clearly L'Étoile was being visited by a little know-it-all.

"Well, I see," Markus said. "Then we'll discuss the menu in peace and quiet with the headwaiter."

"That might be a solution, yes," the cloakroom attendant mumbled.

Right then the girls came out of the bathroom again. They

smelled strongly of perfume. Sigmund stood up and Markus nodded at the cloakroom attendant.

"Markus," he said. "That's my name."

After early indications of a small traffic jam in the doorway, Markus and Sigmund stepped aside and let the girls go in first. The headwaiter was there to receive them. He was a distinguished, older gentleman wearing pinstriped trousers and a dark jacket. He had silvery gray hair and was well over six feet tall. Markus lost a little of his chutzpah. He didn't know headwaiters were so tall.

"Do you have a reservation?" he asked. It didn't seem like he'd noticed that they were kids. He had a slight lisp, and his voice was deep, rich, and restrained.

"Yes," Sigmund said. "Under Markus Simonsen, Junior. Party of four."

Sigmund was the one who had made the reservation, and he hadn't mentioned that he'd made it under Junior's name. Markus noticed that the girls were looking at him in mild astonishment. The headwaiter nodded and led them to a table in the heart of the restaurant.

"I hope this will be all right," he said. "Your waiter will be with you in a moment."

"I'm Markus," Markus said. "That's my name."

"I'm Mr. Dahl," the headwaiter said and disappeared without discussing the menu with them in peace and quiet.

There was a moment of silence. Ellen Christine and Mona were looking at the boys, especially Markus, as if they still couldn't quite believe their own eyes. Markus noticed that they were both wearing makeup. Strictly speaking, he thought makeup was silly, but then of course he had made some slight adjustments to his own appearance. Plus he wasn't Markus anymore, but Markus Junior, and Markus Junior didn't think makeup was silly. He was totally sure of that. The waiter brought their menus. He was young and on the ball.

"Well, boys," he said. "I see you're out with the ladies tonight."

"My name is Markus," Markus imprinted, although the waiter did not appear to be impressed.

"Will you be having apéritifs tonight?" the waiter asked.

"That's not out of the question," Sigmund said. "What do you have?"

"We have champagne, sherry, whisky, Campari, mineral water, orange soda, Coke, fizzy lemonade, juice, and water."

Markus wondered for a moment if he should order champagne, but Sigmund, who understood that the waiter was just trying to be funny, beat him to it.

"Four Cokes. On the rocks."

"Coming right up, sir," the waiter said, walking off briskly.

"What does 'on the rocks' mean?" Ellen Christine asked.

"With ice," Sigmund answered.

He was sitting with his back to the window, next to Ellen Christine. Markus wasn't sure that was actually correct. True, Sigmund was six months older than he, and Ellen Christine was four months older than Mona. And when a younger couple invites an older couple out, the older couple should of course be seated with a view of the room. But Sigmund was actually the one who'd invited everyone and maybe that meant that the younger couple should sit facing the room. He pondered this as he studied the menu. It was big, and his self-confidence was getting smaller and smaller. Their entrance, which had gone quite well, had been rather taxing, and now the names of all the hors d'oeuvres, main courses, and desserts were starting to spin in front of his eyes.

"Now, Markus. What should we choose?" Sigmund said, challenging him.

Markus stared down at the menu. He had no idea. To tell the truth he wasn't hungry at all. He really couldn't imagine eating more than a small piece of pizza, but there was no pizza on the menu.

"I'm not quite sure," he said slowly. "What do you guys want?"

"You decide," Mona said.

"We're not that used to restaurant food," Ellen Christine said. "Pick something you know is good."

Markus nodded. He was sitting with his head bowed, like in the old days. His earlobes were burning, and the bow tie was digging into his neck.

"Yes," Sigmund said. "You don't let guests pick between different dishes at home, so why should you in a restaurant?"

He'd also studied the etiquette book and knew large portions of it by heart. The girls nodded in satisfaction, and Markus mostly felt like wringing his neck.

"Well, have you all decided?"

That was the waiter, here with their Cokes.

All four of them stared at Markus. He jumped right in.

"Four orders of the *anchois vinaigrettes*, four orders of *boeuf bourguignon*, and four orange soufflés."

He had randomly picked items from the menu figuring that the best food would be the things with the hardest names. He pronounced the names of the different dishes at a furious pace, exactly the way they were spelled on paper. It seemed like that wasn't entirely correct, because the waiter looked a little confused.

"Could you please repeat that?"

Markus did so.

"What is bo-ee-uff?" the waiter asked.

Markus pointed at the menu.

"Ah, that's pronounced *buhf*. It's a French dish made with beef."

"I know that, but I usually just call it bo-ee-uff."

"Why?"

"It's easier," Markus said and cleared his throat.

He was starting to feel a tickle in his nose. How were you supposed to sneeze in a restaurant? As quietly as possible and with your face turned away?

"Bo-ee-uff," the waiter mumbled as he jotted down the order. "I'll remember that. What would you like to drink with your meal?"

Markus shot Sigmund a distressed look as he tried to hold back his sneeze. Luckily Sigmund picked up on the sign and proved to be both a very polished restaurant guest and a good friend.

"Juice with the hors d'oeuvres, Coke with the main course, and fizzy lemonade with the desserts."

"What vintage?" the waiter asked.

"You're a real funny guy," Sigmund said.

The waiter nodded.

"You guys aren't so bad yourselves."

Then Markus sneezed. A half-suppressed sneeze with his face toward the waiter. Tears streamed out of his eyes, and the tickling sensation in his nose was still there. The waiter discreetly dried a few drops off his cheek and quickly left the table, just in time to miss hearing a faint voice whisper:

"I'm Markus."

After getting off to such a good start, it wasn't that surprising to encounter a minor setback. Markus's sneezing fit was a major setback. It was one of those attacks that never ends. Mons was the same way. When he started sneezing, he could keep going for half an hour, at least. Sometimes they would start sneezing simultaneously and have a good laugh about it afterwards. Nobody was laughing now. Quite the contrary, both of the girls and Sigmund were pretending they hadn't noticed it. They were eagerly discussing books they'd read, movies they'd seen, teachers they disliked, and tennis matches they'd won. But the whole time they were secretly keeping an eye on him, waiting for the next sneeze. Each time he sneezed, Mona would lean over the table casually. As if she'd just thought of something to say, or as if she were especially interested in something that someone else had just said. After his fourteenth sneeze, the attack was over. The part in his hair was no longer neat, and his red handkerchief was full of green and yellow blotches. The waiter brought their juice and the *anchois*. The setback continued.

Anchois vinaigrette is considered a lovely appetizer and a delightful dish to consume out on a terrace in the summertime, but there are very few thirteen-year-olds who consider it their favorite dish. It consists of anchovies, minced hard-boiled egg, minced onion, minced parsley, and dressing. It's quite salty.

"THAT'S *anchois vinaigrette*?" Ellen Christine asked, eyeing her plate in suspicion.

"Yup," Markus said, bravely putting an anchovy filet into his mouth. It was slimy and slippery, and he had the sense that it was alive. What he wanted most of all was to spit it out, but he slurped it down like a strand of spaghetti.

"Delicious," he moaned and drank his juice in a single gulp.

"You can have mine too," Mona said.

"And mine," Ellen Christine said. "We're on a diet."

"You guys should be careful with that," Sigmund said. "Dieting can be dangerous."

Sigmund liked grown-up food. He ate his *anchois vinaigrette* slowly and with a healthy appetite. Markus watched him gratefully.

"We just want to save room for the main course," Ellen Christine said.

"Yes," Mona said, "for the bo-ee-uff."

She dumped her anchovies onto Markus's plate.

"Thanks," he said, smiling wanly but charmingly.

Ellen Christine passed her plate across the table. Sigmund glanced up from his anchovies, smiled at Markus, and said, "You lucky dog."

"You can have these if you want," Markus said.

Sigmund shook his head.

"No thanks. It's a little too fishy for me. My taste buds aren't as mature as yours."

The girls nodded eagerly and expressed their admiration for how grown-up Markus's taste buds were. That decided it. With a silent sigh, he took the plate Ellen Christine had passed him and dumped the contents onto his own plate. Now there were fourteen anchovy filets lying there. They looked like a sliced-up octopus. He ate them in silence under the admiring gaze of his friends. When the last filet swam down his throat, all the others wanted to come back up again. He swallowed and swallowed and somehow or other managed to drown them in stomach acid. Then the waiter arrived with their *boeuf.*

Boeuf bourguignon is a classic French dish that can contain a variety of good ingredients. Although it is made with red wine, children can eat it because the alcohol evaporates while it cooks. The dish L'Étoile served contained beef, carrots, celery, onion, garlic, tomato purée, bacon, and mushrooms. It was a hearty dish that the waiter served with saffron rice. The portions were large, and the waiter assured them that there was more where that had come from.

"That's good," Ellen Christine said, nodding toward Markus, "because he eats like a horse."

"Small man, big stomach, huh?" the waiter said, winking at Ellen Christine.

"Could I please have a glass of water?" Markus asked.

He had no idea how he was going to make it through all that meat, but at least he had the strength left to say "No thank you" when the waiter tried to give him a second helping. That was actually all he was able to say. He tried to loosen his cummerbund, but it was held on by a hook-and-loop closure that he couldn't access because it was under the tuxedo jacket. Then the waiter

brought the orange soufflé. An enormous dessert. It looked like
a huge, swollen sponge cake covered with powdered sugar. It was
made of flour, butter, milk, sugar, orange peel, orange extract, and
eggs. It was hot out of the oven and the pride of L'Étoile. The girls
were delighted, Sigmund was relaxed, and Markus felt like Homer
Simpson after he'd eaten one too many doughnuts. He guided his
spoon slowly down toward the soufflé, emitted a gurgling sound,
sort of a mixture between a burp and a belch, and got up slowly,
like an old man, from the table.

"Excuse me," he muttered without opening his mouth.

He walked quickly with short steps through the restaurant and
out to the bathroom, where he rid himself of twelve anchovy filets,
eight strips of bacon, four pearl onions, two ounces of beef, and
a handkerchief in a variety of colors. When he emerged, walking
back through the cloakroom, he was feeling fairly dizzy.

The cloakroom attendant glanced up from his newspaper.

"You're the one named Markus, right?"

Markus opened his mouth to respond, closed it, nodded, and
ran back into the bathroom.

"You're sure fond of that bathroom, aren't you?" the cloakroom
attendant said when he came out again.

"Simonsen," Markus said. "Markus Simonsen, Junior."

"I see," the attendant said. "I thought it was senior."

When he got back to his seat, the others had finished eating,
and the waiter was standing next to the table.

"Your soufflé has gotten cold," he said.

"That doesn't matter," Markus said. "I'm not going to have any."

The waiter raised his eyebrows.

"Our soufflé isn't to your liking?"

Markus had had enough now. He looked the waiter right in the eyes and in a burst of courageous desperation said:

"I have invited guests to a restaurant. What can I expect from the headwaiter and the wait staff?"

"Heh?" the waiter said, but Markus kept going, in a loud, deadpan voice as if he were reciting something he'd memorized and, actually, that was exactly what he was doing:

"First and foremost I can expect polite—and not in any way condescending—attentiveness. The headwaiter and the wait staff's most important duty is to make sure the guests are happy, and the biggest blunder they can commit is ignoring the guests or making them feel inferior. A skillful waiter knows precisely when he's needed at a table without your having to call him over, but he's never intrusive. He does not repeatedly ask if you are enjoying your meal, and he does not correct you if you are so misfortunate as to mispronounce the name of a French wine!"

That hit home. The girls looked at him, speechless and full of admiration. Sigmund eagerly took notes on his notepad, and the waiter stared at him while opening and closing his mouth like a fish that had suddenly found itself on dry land. Sigmund put his notepad into his pocket and smiled at the waiter.

"And now we'd like the check, please. If that isn't too much trouble."

The waiter nodded and retreated quickly and silently.

"That served him right," Ellen Christine said.

Mona nodded enthusiastically and said, "That was the coolest thing I've ever heard."

"I'm just not going to put up with any of it," Markus said, groping around for the handkerchief he'd left in the bathroom. The waiter came back with their check. He set it in front of Markus without a word and withdrew quickly and discreetly. Markus looked at it and pushed it over to Sigmund. It was for exactly two hundred and fifty dollars. Sigmund got up slowly.

"Excuse us a second," he said. "We just have to go …" He glanced over at Markus and then continued, "comb our hair."

"I didn't think it would be so much!"

Sigmund had just splashed some water on his face. He dried himself off with one of the hand towels that were lying in neat piles next to the sink.

"How much do you have, Sigmund?"

Markus was standing next to him, flushed and agitated. This was absolutely the worst thing that could happen. And to him, the kid who'd just chewed out the waiter! They really couldn't count on getting much sympathy from him.

"A hundred and fifty."

"You have to call your dad!"

"There's no way. He'll freak out if he finds out that I spent my savings on a restaurant. Plus I think you ought to pay for some of it too."

"I only have twenty dollars!"

"Then you have to call your dad."

"No!"

"I'll do it."

Markus sighed heavily. He was sure that Mons would help them out of the crisis, but he wasn't sure what he'd say afterwards.

Well, he'd worry about that when the time came. It really was the only way out, and at least it was a bit of a comfort that Sigmund was going to handle the practical details. They went back to the table, where the waiter stood waiting.

"We have a small problem," Sigmund said.

The waiter looked at him questioningly.

"Unfortunately, we seem to have confused a hundred-dollar bill with a ten-dollar bill."

The waiter seemed strangely agitated.

"Aha," he said.

"And that means we've only brought a hundred and seventy dollars with us."

The waiter smiled broadly.

"I'll get the headwaiter."

The headwaiter wasn't smiling. He wasn't six feet tall either. He was twelve feet tall! And his hair was gray like granite.

"You can't pay for your meal?" he asked slowly.

"Um, we're just going to go to the bathroom," the girls said in unison, getting up quickly.

"That's my understanding," the waiter said. He was standing behind the headwaiter and seemed to be enjoying himself.

"You'll get the money, no problem," Sigmund said.

"That's good to hear," the headwaiter said.

"I think so too," the waiter said.

"If we could borrow a phone, we'll call Mr. Simonsen, Senior. Then he'll come and pay, and then the whole thing will be settled."

The headwaiter brought a cell phone and handed it to Sigmund. Markus stared down at the table, feeling like an anchovy.

"Hello, Mr. Simonsen? This is Sigmund. I'm sitting here with Junior. Yes, Markus. Now listen up, Mr. Simonsen. We are at L'Étoile. What? Yes, L'Étoile, the restaurant. What? Yes. L'Étoile. What? No, we're just sitting here having a good time, sort of, but now there's a little problem."

After being interrupted numerous times by a very surprised Mons, Sigmund finally managed to explain that they needed eighty-five more dollars to pay their bill.

"It's all set," he told the headwaiter.

"Give me the phone."

Sigmund gave it to him.

"This is Mr. Dahl. What? Yes. Then it's settled, Mr. Simonsen. No, no, it's no trouble at all. What? Well, yes, as far as I understand it, they've had a really nice time."

He hung up the phone and smiled at Markus. He was back to being six feet tall again.

"Well, boys, everything worked out for the best. Your dad will be here within the hour."

"Yeah, I'm sure he will," Markus said.

And then there was dancing. Or uncoordinated gymnastics or aerobics or whatever you would call the strange movements Markus was making on the dance floor with Mona in tow. He didn't care that the other couples were looking at them in surprise. He didn't even notice Sigmund trying to gesture to him to tone it down a little. The evening was already a complete fiasco. Soon his dad would be here to get him. It really couldn't get any worse than it already was, but at least he could show them a dance they would never forget. And he succeeded. He'd seen a cartoon where Donald and Daisy

Duck had danced without having to touch each other. He started mimicking it. His legs moved like drumsticks as he bounced around the room, his back straight, his knees bent, his hands flat as if he were paddling through the air, all the while jutting his head in and out like a piston. Mona tried to grab hold of his hands. He clenched them into fists and then pointed his two index fingers at his partner, just like Donald Duck had done. Then he started swinging his arms, back and forth in time with the chicken-like movements of his head, as he smiled charmingly. Mona was backing up, anxiously staring at the index finger plunging forward and stopping just an inch from her eyes, where it would hang quivering in the air for a second before it was pulled back and the next index finger would take its place. Markus had danced them into a corner of the room. He stood there jumping up and down, his index fingers jabbing at a furious pace, like the needle on a sewing machine. The other guests kept dancing, but you really couldn't blame them for taking an interest in the couple in the corner. And it just got more and more interesting. Markus had seen a lot of cartoons and had taken particular notice of an eye-catching dance he'd once seen in a Russian one. Suddenly he leapt up into the air, kicking both feet out as if he were trying to do a split. Then he squatted down and rested his weight on his hands behind his back while he tried to kick first one leg and then the other straight out in front of him without losing his balance. He looked like some kind of spastic crab. With each kick he shouted, "Hey!"

The Polish dance band had finished the fast song, and the singer started singing, "I just called to say I love you ..."

Markus stood up, bowed politely and reached for Mona with

his hands. She pressed herself back against the wall, staring at Markus in terror.

"Thanks for the dance," she whispered.

"Don't you want to dance anymore?"

"I can't dance the way you can," she said softly. "No one can."

Markus searched for a second for a suitable quote from the book and found one.

"Young people have their own style," he said calmly.

They walked back to the table, where Sigmund was sitting and eagerly taking notes on his notepad while Ellen Christine drank lemonade and made puppy-dog eyes at Sigmund.

"What dance were you guys doing?" she asked when they reached the table.

"A modern one," Markus said.

"It was incredible. What's it called?"

He thought for a moment.

"It's called the Markuska," he said.

"So this is where you're sitting and enjoying yourselves!" said Mons, who had just walked up to the table.

He was wearing a pair of old flannel pants, a faded shirt, and a gray jacket with leather patches on the elbows. He really stuck out quite a bit compared to all of L'Étoile's other diners, who were all dressed up for a night on the town. The mood at the table was subdued and unhappy.

"Yeah," Ellen Christine said.

"We've been having a great time," Mona said.

"That's good to hear," Mons said. "They almost wouldn't let me in."

"Yes, well," Sigmund said kindly, "your outfit is maybe not quite …" He stopped mid-sentence. Sometimes even Sigmund knew when it was a good idea to shut up.

The waiter and the headwaiter came over to them. Mons paid the rest of the bill. Everyone said thank you. The waiter and the headwaiter disappeared.

"Would you like a soda, Mr. Simonsen?" Sigmund asked.

"I'm going to drive you guys home," Mons said, heading out to the cloakroom.

All four of them stood up. Markus forgot to pull the chair out for Mona, but she managed on her own. Mons got out some money to pay for the coat check, but the attendant said:

"There's no need, sir. The young man named Markus asked me to include the coat fee on his dinner check."

"Oh, he did, did he?" Mons said, stepping out onto the sidewalk to breathe some fresh air.

"Is that your father?" the attendant asked as he passed Markus his silk scarf. Markus nodded.

"You're really spoiled, aren't you?"

Markus didn't respond.

"If I were your father, I'd spend a little more money on myself. Not just on you. He needs a new jacket."

Not much was said in the car. When the girls were dropped off they said, "Thank you very much," and that they'd had the time of their lives. And when Sigmund got out of the car, he reached out to shake hands with Mons.

"Thank you so much, Mr. Simonsen. I'll never forget this."

"Me neither," Mons said. "Your parents won't either, for that matter. I called them and told them where you were."

"Um, can I sleep at your house tonight, Markus?" Sigmund asked.

But nobody heard him because Mons had already put the old Lada in gear, and father and son were on their way home to a very unhappy conversation.

After receiving a thorough introduction to his father's financial situation, Markus was sent to bed. He himself suggested that, as punishment for his extravagant expenditure, he could go to bed without any supper. Mons didn't think that was funny. He wasn't mad; he almost never was. But he was resigned in a way that reminded Markus of how his mother used to get when he did something wrong. That was even worse. For a second Markus felt like telling him everything: about the letters, the fan club, the training he had to complete before he met Diana Mortensen in Horten. Maybe his dad would understand, maybe not. He never found out, because he didn't tell him any of it.

"Good night," he mumbled and went to his room. He had both a stomachache and a headache.

He fell asleep and dreamed that he got in a fight with a doorman, a waiter, and a headwaiter who were actually monsters instead of people.

"We'll teach you some manners, you little pipsqueak!" the doorman monster snarled.

"Death to the rude!" shouted the waiter monster.

"We'll make mincemeat out of him," lisped the headwaiter monster, "*Boeuf soufflé Markus vinaigrette!*"

When he woke up it was one thirty in the morning. He was

dripping with sweat. He got out of bed and went to the bathroom, where he drank a liter of water and messed up the last remnants of the tired part in his hair. He stood there and stared at himself in the mirror until he felt like he could recognize his own face again. Mons appeared behind him. He looked at Markus a little shyly. He was clearly sorry, exactly the way Mom used to be after she'd been mad or resigned.

Dad is two people now, Markus thought without knowing why. He knew he could take the easy way out and leave all the work to his dad. He would almost certainly offer an unnecessary apology, but his dad wasn't the one who should apologize. He was.

"I'm sorry, Dad. I'll never do it again," he said, still facing the mirror.

The relief Mons felt filled the whole bathroom.

"Do what? Go to L'Étoile?"

"No. Be so terribly charming."

Mons picked up a towel and handed it to him.

"That's good to hear."

Markus spent the rest of the night lying next to Mons on his mom's side of the double bed. It had been a long time since he'd slept there, and he knew that this might be the last time. He was thirteen years old. His dad lay there next to him pretending to be asleep. And it was really nice.

CHAPTER 11 Two weeks went by without their hearing anything from Diana Mortensen. Mona called every day for the first week, but Markus didn't want to see her and came up with different excuses until she stopped calling. The Help Diana Club was still holding its meetings at the stone quarry, but they were somehow a little tamer than before. Markus had returned *The Guide to Good Manners in the '90s* to the library and had refused to learn the rules of golf. He and Mons had started planning their trip to Denmark. Diana Mortensen seemed less and less real.

One week before they were going to leave, the letter was sitting there in the mailbox. A blue envelope with an American stamp. To Mr. Markus Simonsen. He opened it as if it were a time bomb, read it four times, used the comb in an unsuccessful attempt to part his hair in the middle, and called Sigmund. Half an hour later, he was sitting under the tarp and trying to keep his hands from shaking while Sigmund read:

> *Dear Markus,*
>
> *Thank you so much for your last letter. You're so lucky to have a son. I'm very fond of children. I was in a soap commercial with a little boy named Melvin Henderson. A real little bundle of charm and very talented. When you wrote about Markus Junior, it made me think of him. I'm sure they'd have*

become the best of friends if they'd met each other. But of course they never will. Isn't life random? That you wrote to me, for example, and that I'm going to be in Horten and maybe meet you. I arrive August 3rd and will stay for a while. I'm not in The Rich and the Powerful *anymore. I had a falling out with the producer and told him straight out what I thought about his stupid show, so he had the writers write me out of it. I fall to my death from a skyscraper during a pro-environment rally. But it's for the best. You see, I just don't have a dishonest bone in my body. I always say flat out what I mean, and if they can't respect me for who I am, then who needs them. And can you imagine, Markus, it all started with a silly disagreement about money. You see, Billy earns almost twice as much as me just because he's so well known. Everyone just thinks about money here in Hollywood. I'm sure you'll read about it in the papers at home, because the episode where I fall to my death from the skyscraper is going to air in Norway next week. Please don't believe everything they write, Markus! They spread so many false rumors—it's unbearable! My agent says quitting* The Rich and the Powerful *is just a good career move. The show's ratings are falling, and the viewership is taking a nosedive. I'm happy because I quit while I was ahead. I have a lot of offers, but I don't know what I'll choose. At the moment I'm working on an extremely exciting mouthwash commercial. I start out sad, then I gargle with the mouthwash, and then I smile. It's a fun role, and I go through the transition from sad to happy in just 20 seconds. Maybe you'll see the ads in Norway this fall.*

Well, as you can see, I have plenty to keep me busy, but

every now and then I dream of getting away from it all. And now that dream will come true. I'm very happy about that and will be even happier if my second dream comes true as well. The dream of meeting you. And hopefully your son too. I am, as I said, very fond of children. Yes, dear Markus, as you can see, my life is a total mess right now. But I'll be in Horten on August 3rd. Well, think of me once in a while!

Yours, Diana

Sigmund looked up from the letter. He smiled contentedly.

"I knew it! Diana, here we come!"

Markus regretted having shown the letter to Sigmund, but he was just like Diana. He didn't have a dishonest bone in his body.

"I can't meet her."

"Why not?"

"I … I'm going to be in Denmark."

"You have to tell your dad that you want to go to Horten instead."

"No one goes to Horten for vacation."

"Sure they do. There are lots of tourist attractions in Horten."

"Like what?"

"The Naval Museum, for example. They have a lot of nice statues."

"Of who?"

"Of Captain Oscar Wisting, one of the guys who went to the South Pole with Roald Amundsen."

"How did you know that?"

"I've been reading up on Horten. You should too. There's also a nice museum of photography there. And a museum that has classic cars. Your dad will like that. He has quite a classic car himself, doesn't he?"

"He does not. It's just a little old."

"We can stay at the Grand Ocean. It's a golf hotel."

"I told you, I refuse to play golf."

"You don't have to play golf to stay at a golf hotel."

"I can't be Markus Simonsen, Junior."

"Sure you can. You were amazing at L'Étoile."

"I had a stomachache for a week after that."

"Be yourself then."

"Huh?"

"She says she doesn't have a dishonest bone in her body, doesn't she? I'm sure that means she likes honest people."

"Um, hello? I haven't been honest."

"No, but now you will be. Her letter made you realize that honesty is the best policy."

"No!"

"Plus, she's fond of children."

"She won't be fond of them anymore once she meets me."

"Just relax. I'll be right nearby the whole time. If something goes wrong, I'll intervene."

Markus was about to ask how Sigmund was planning to intervene, but Sigmund had already moved on.

"Now let's go home and talk to your dad."

"But …"

"Don't you trust me?"

"Sure, but …"

"Good. Then we agree."

"Why do you always get to have the last word?"

"Because I'm always right," Sigmund said, getting up to leave.

"Do you play golf, Mr. Simonsen?"

"No, but it might be fun to give it a try."

"Yeah, wouldn't it? You ought to treat yourself to a vacation at the Grand Ocean Hotel, Norway's premier golfing resort."

Markus, Sigmund, and Mons were sitting around the kitchen table at Markus's house eating lunch. Markus had hoped that Sigmund would start by just blurting out the idea of going to Horten on vacation. Then without a doubt Mons would have just said no, and that would have been the end of it. But Sigmund was smarter than that.

"You don't say?" Mons said.

"Yeah," Sigmund said. "It's in the heart of Norway's golf country. It's less than an hour's drive from there to the golf courses at Vestfold, Kjekstad, Borregaard, Skjeberg, Onsøy, Bogstad, and Drøbak."

"You don't say!"

Mons looked at Sigmund, interested. Markus fidgeted uncomfortably. Sigmund could tell that the fish had noticed the bait and kept going:

"You could spend a couple of days playing at the unbelievably posh Borre Golf Club."

"Yeah, that might be fun," Mons said. "Would you like some more hot chocolate, Sigmund?"

"Yes, please. Borre Golf Club offers an inviting golfing environment for established players, novices, and visitors of all ages! And the Grand Ocean Hotel will be happy to help you arrange the practical details, such as discounted greens fees, tee-time reservations, and caddy arrangements."

Mons gave him a slightly surprised look and asked, "Tell me, Sigmund. Do your parents have some kind of a financial interest in this hotel?"

"Oh no, Mr. Simonsen. I just get so carried away when I talk about it. A game of golf in the exquisite beauty of the Norwegian countryside. What more could you want?"

Markus sensed that Sigmund was about to take things too far, but his friend was in complete control. He could make the most unnatural sentences sound completely natural. If he didn't become an astrophysicist, he could certainly have a brilliant career in advertising. Mons smiled at Markus.

"Maybe we should consider that for next summer?"

"Consider it now!" Sigmund said enthusiastically. "The Grand Ocean Hotel has a hundred comfortably appointed rooms with a guest marina, ample parking, outstanding food, and great service at reasonable prices."

"We're going to Denmark this year," Mons said, "but thanks for the tip."

Sigmund was unstoppable.

"Why spend your vacation in a foreign country when the golf courses are so fresh and green here at home?"

Surely by now his father must realize that something else was going on. Nope.

"You've got a point, but you know Markus and I have been

looking forward to our trip to Tivoli Amusement Park in Copenhagen."

"I bet he'd much rather go to the Grand Ocean Hotel. Isn't that so, Markus?"

Markus had been sitting quietly, picking at his food while Sigmund went on and on. Right to the very end, he had hoped that his dad would come down in favor of Denmark. He'd really been looking forward to going to Tivoli. He had even held out a faint hope that he would have enough courage to ride the roller coaster. That would have been something to tell his new classmates about, before they started calling him Wormster. "I went to Tivoli over the summer. The roller coaster was so great I almost didn't want to get off." That would have been a nice start to three long years of junior high. But now Sigmund had hooked his dad and handed the fishing rod to Markus. All he had to do was reel his dad in.

"It doesn't matter to me," he said.

This way he left the decision up to his dad, and at the same time, showed Sigmund that he wasn't going along with this voluntarily, but under duress. Mons looked at him in surprise.

"Really?"

"Sure. You decide, Dad," he said bravely. Just send me to the North Pole, or wherever you two want. It doesn't matter to me, he thought.

"Well, it would be cheaper of course," Mons said. "Maybe it's a good idea."

"It's a great idea," Sigmund said. "Can I come?"

"Yeah, if your parents say it's all right," Mons said.

"I'm sure they will. I can't wait."

"Well, it's a plan, then," Mons said, looking pleased. "Where is that golf hotel?"

"It's in Horten," Markus mumbled.

Mons looked at them wide-eyed. A fish on land that didn't understand how it got there.

"Horten? Where the old Navy shipyard is?"

"With a special putting green on the roof, where you can warm up before your tee time and practice your putt," Sigmund said quickly. "I'll call home and ask if I can go."

Sigmund's parents were anxious, not without reason, that their son would grow up too quickly and miss out on his childhood. After all he was only thirteen years old, even though he talked like a grown-up. It reassured them some that his best friend was shy little Markus, who was a few months younger than him to boot. So it didn't even occur to them to say no when Sigmund asked if he could go to Horten with Markus and his dad. Mons was also glad the boys were friends. He was afraid Markus would turn into some kind of loner, but he was obviously flourishing with Sigmund. Maybe he was flourishing a little faster than Mons would have liked. But flourishing was flourishing, Mons figured.

Sigmund spent the whole day there and enthusiastically took charge of planning their Horten trip. He pulled out a couple of glossy brochures that he happened to have in his pocket. Mons read them with interest. In the brochures he discovered exactly the same sentences that Sigmund had used when he'd lavished praise on the Grand Ocean Hotel earlier. Mons was somewhat relieved to find that the boy hadn't come up with all that fancy phrasing on his own, but had memorized it word for word from a brochure. That made him somehow a little more normal. He reserved a double room and a single room at the golf hotel and was already looking forward to trying to swing a golf club. He considered golf a fairly risk-free sport. The worst that could happen was getting hit in the head by a golf ball, but even Mons didn't think that was very likely.

That evening all three of them sat on the sofa with some soda and potato chips to watch the weekly episode of *The Rich and the Powerful*.

Rebecca Jones stood on the narrow ledge outside the open window of a skyscraper. The sign she was holding over her head said STOP THE MADNESS. She looked sadder than ever. The crowd on the street down below looked like tiny Lilliputians. That made sense since the window she was standing in front of was on the sixty-eighth floor.

"She should have picked a lower window," Mons said. "No one can read what it says on her sign."

Neither Markus nor Sigmund said anything. They were helping themselves to the potato chips mechanically and at a furious pace.

"They would have to have binoculars to read what that says," Mons continued.

"Now she's going to fall down," Markus whispers.

"No, no," Mons said reassuringly. "Stuff like that only happens in real life. Not on TV."

"You want to bet?" Sigmund asked, without taking his eyes off the screen.

"Bet? Bet on what?"

"On whether she falls down or not."

"Sure. Why not? How about fifty cents?"

"No. A nice dinner at Fishland."

"What?"

"The fancy seafood restaurant at the Grand Ocean. By the marina in Horten. If she falls down, you pay. If she doesn't fall down, I pay."

Mons looked over at the TV screen. Rebecca Jones was still standing outside the window. He felt like playing a little trick on Sigmund, to get him back. He was sure that Sigmund was the one who had talked Markus into their crazy visit to L'Étoile. And now the boy wanted to go out for another feast. Mons smiled to himself. This could really be fun. When Rebecca climbed back into the skyscraper, he would fling up his arms apologetically and say that he was afraid it was really going to cost Sigmund, but a deal's a deal and a promise is a promise. This could be a little lesson to him. Of course they wouldn't actually eat the fancy dinner, but he wouldn't reveal that until they got to Horten. Then he would give them a little talk about the dangers of gambling and take the boys out for pizza instead.

"It's a deal," he said. "I hope you can afford it."

Right as he said that, Diana Mortensen fell off the skyscraper, dropping like a rag doll.

Although Markus had been prepared for what happened, he jumped. He had to close his eyes for a second. When he opened them, Diana Mortensen was lying facedown on the asphalt. Markus felt an intense wave of hatred for the stingy producer.

"I can't believe they did that," he said softly.

Mons stared at Sigmund, his eyes wide, his mouth agape. "But … but … how did you know that …?" he stammered.

"We had a hunch," Sigmund said. "I believe you lost the bet."

"But … but … I didn't think … I mean … we weren't really betting, were we?"

Sigmund gave him a reproachful look.

"A deal's a deal, Mr. Simonsen, and a promise is a promise."

CHAPTER 12 August first. The Bastø ferry was on its way across the Oslo Fjord from Moss to Horten. It was full of truck drivers, tourists, and other people going on vacation or coming back from vacation. It had been pouring down rain for five days throughout eastern Norway, and the mood onboard was a little low. Seated in the cafeteria's smoking section was Mons Simonsen, who without knowing it himself, was identical to millionaire and mountain climber Markus Simonsen, Senior. He was drinking black coffee, smoking his pipe, and wondering how he had actually ended up here. Seated in the non-smoking section was his son, Markus, a.k.a. Markus Junior, along with his friend Sigmund. They had agreed that Markus would just be a *little* honest. He would pretend that he was Markus Junior, but he wouldn't curl his hair or pretend he had mastered *The Guide to Good Manners in the '90s*. He would be himself. A completely normal millionaire's son.

Sigmund thought it would be best this way. Sure, he could fool Mona and Ellen Christine into thinking he was a little gentleman, but Diana Mortensen probably knew a ton of sophisticated teenagers and would probably notice that there was something a little awkward about his politeness. An audacious, slightly disheveled millionaire's son was more plausible, Sigmund said. Markus had retorted that he didn't feel audacious or disheveled. That was almost worse than happy and charming.

"What about the silent, thoughtful type?" Sigmund had asked. "That's what you are, after all."

"I'm not silent and thoughtful. I'm shy and confused."

"But you seem silent and thoughtful. That's what makes you so exciting."

Even though Markus knew Sigmund was just flattering him to get him to go along with the plan, he felt a jolt of pleasure. Silent and thoughtful. Yeah, maybe that's what he was.

He stared out at the fjord and the rain making stripes down the windows. The trip from Moss to Horten took forty minutes. It was pretty windy, and the Bastø ferry was rocking back and forth through the waves. Markus was silent, thoughtful, and a little queasy. He was probably one of the first people to ever manage to get seasick on the short trip from Moss to Horten. That was also setting a kind of record, you know.

"Don't you want the rest of your soda?" Sigmund asked.

Markus quickly made his way to the bathroom, but he wasn't sick enough to actually throw up. When he came back, Mons was standing by the table.

"Well, boys. It's about time to head back down to the car."

It was cool down on the car deck. It smelled like oil, gasoline, and diesel fuel. That didn't help the queasiness. They got into the car and waited for their turn to drive ashore. Mons put the key in the ignition.

"I think I'm going to throw up," said Markus, who was sitting in the front seat next to his dad.

"A plastic bag!" Mons shouted. "Sigmund, is there a plastic bag back there?"

"No," Sigmund said.

"Urg," Markus said.

The cars were starting to move ahead of them.

"Try to hold it until we get ashore!" Mons said, trying to start the car. It didn't start.

"Come on," he muttered desperately, turning the key again. The engine made a noise that sounded like a small cough. The cars behind them started honking. Markus gulped.

"Roll down the window!" Mons shouted, turning the key one more time. "Don't throw up in the car! Ah, it started that time. I just had it in the wrong gear. Hold on, Markus! We'll be off the boat in a sec!"

The car slowly rolled off the ferry. Markus sat with his head out the window. He swallowed and swallowed as they drove past the man directing the line of cars. Then they were in Horten. He'd survived the voyage without throwing up, and in two days he would meet Diana Mortensen.

Mons got a single room with a view of the parking lot, and the boys got a double room with a view of the marina. They prepared for their big meeting as they unpacked.

"OK. I'm Diana," Sigmund said. "You're you. You're meeting me for the first time. What do you say?"

"I don't think I say anything. I'm kind of more silent and thoughtful."

"You have to say something. You can't be silent and thoughtful the whole time."

"Well, then I guess I say, hi," Markus said.

"Yeah. And then?"

"And then I guess I ask if … she had a good trip. Maybe."

"Do it!"

"What?"

"Ask me if I had a good trip."

"But you have no idea how her trip was."

"How dumb can you be? I'm Diana. Right?"

"OK. Hi."

"Who are you?"

"Why are you asking that? You know perfectly well who I am."

"Yes, but Diana doesn't know."

"Oh, right."

"Who are you?"

"I'm not just going to come out and say that," Markus whispered.

"Huh?"

"I'm going to be myself, right? And if I'm myself, I'm definitely not going to be brave enough to say who I am. It's too embarrassing."

"Say who you are!"

"I'm Markus Junior," Markus mumbled.

"Oh, it's you!" Sigmund said, beaming. "I've been looking forward to meeting you so much. We have so much to talk about."

"How was your trip?" Markus asked hoarsely.

"The trip was fine. It's wonderful to be back in Norway again. Your father's told me so much about you."

Markus searched desperately for something to say, but the only thing he could think of was:

"My name is Markus."

"You don't have to say that twice."

"I want to imprint it. My name is Markus."

"Forget etiquette. Be yourself."

"I can't go through with it," Markus said unhappily.

"You're the one who wanted to do this."

"I don't think I can be myself after all."

"Who do you want to be then?"

"I'd really prefer to be no one," Markus said quietly.

Sigmund sighed.

"You can't back out now. Do you have any workout clothes with you?"

"I brought my tracksuit."

"Put it on."

"Why?"

"Maybe you'll feel more relaxed wearing it."

"I can't meet Diana Mortensen in a tracksuit!"

"Sure you can. Lots of millionaires wear tracksuits."

Markus put it on.

"Now walk back and forth."

Markus did as he was told. He didn't feel any more relaxed. "How do I look?" he asked nervously.

"Not too bad, but something's missing."

"I know."

"Put this on."

Sigmund pulled a black cap out of his suitcase. It said GOLFER.

"I refuse," Markus said, and then put the cap on.

"Turn it around backward."

"Why?"

"It's much cooler."

Markus turned the cap around.

"Good. Walk back and forth again. Cool and casual."

He followed Sigmund's instructions. At first it didn't go that well, but Sigmund was a patient teacher who gave his student a lot of encouragement.

"Yes, would you look at that? Yes! That's much better. Now I'm Diana. What do you say?"

"My name is Markus."

"No!"

"Do you know how much a tennis ball weighs?"

"OK," Sigmund said slowly. "Now we're going to try something else. Put on your suit."

Markus had brought a dark suit, a white dress shirt, and a tie that he was going to wear when they ate dinner at Fishland. He put it on.

"How do I look?" he asked nervously.

"Styling. Now walk."

"Where should I walk?"

"Back and forth. Yes, like that. Wonderful. Very debonair. Say something!"

"What should I say?"

"Whatever. Just talk. Pretend you're the son of a millionaire who always wears a suit."

"I can't pull that off."

"You can pull that off. Just feel the suit. Exactly like what you do when you write letters. Come on."

Slowly Markus started to talk. Haltingly at first, then more and more effortlessly. He let the words pour out of his mouth without thinking, like when he gave the talk about glacier hiking or wrote his autograph letters, and as he spoke, he discovered that he wasn't Markus Simonsen anymore. He was Junior. He expounded on the natural beauty of Norway, which he loved, about funny things that had happened at school, about his envious classmates who had less spending money than he did, exciting tennis matches where he had just barely won at the last possible instant, interesting trips to exotic countries, the annoying paparazzi that chased after Markus Senior, and the loneliness of being different. Because, in the end, that's what he was. A different millionaire's son. And what was strange was that it didn't feel like he was faking it. It felt totally real. He wasn't pretending to be Markus Simonsen, Junior. He *was* Markus Simonsen, Junior. The words came to him all on their own. He just channeled them and passed them on, as he trudged back and forth across the floor of the hotel room. Sometimes thoughtfully with his hands clasped behind his back, other times excitedly, gesticulating effusively. Finally he came to a stop in front of Sigmund and looked him in the eyes as he smiled sorrowfully.

"You know, Diana," Markus Junior said. "Sometimes I wish I were a completely ordinary boy. Do you know what I mean?"

Sigmund nodded mutely. He was completely enthralled. To be sure, he had hoped that he would be able to coax Markus out of his shell, but he never dreamed he would see such an astounding transformation.

"How was that?" Markus asked anxiously. In less than a second, he was himself again.

"That was … totally amazing."

"Do you mean it?"

"That was the most compelling thing I've ever seen. How did you do that?"

"I don't know. It just kind of happened."

Sigmund nodded energetically.

"I understand," he said.

Markus knew that he didn't understand. Of course Sigmund was much better at thinking than he was, but he didn't have enough imagination to understand that for Markus, everything got much easier when he managed to stop thinking. When he thought, it was like everything got all jumbled up, just like at dance class. But when he didn't think, it was as if he became a completely different person from the one he really was. He couldn't explain it, but he knew that that's what it was like. It wasn't hard at all. It was almost uncanny how easy it was. Once he managed to escape from himself, everything was easy.

"I think it's because I'm much better at not being myself than at being myself," he said slowly.

"Uh huh," Sigmund said. "I'm sure that's the explanation. Yeah."

He said it a little sarcastically, and Markus knew that was because he was feeling a little unsure of himself.

"It's not that hard," Markus said encouragingly. "Do you want to try?"

Sigmund looked at the clock.

"Another time. Your dad's waiting for us in the lobby."

Markus nodded. He felt rather content, but at the same time he had an awful taste in his mouth. It was probably a little of the nausea from the ferry ride that was still with him.

When they left the room, Sigmund held the door open for Markus and let him go out first. It felt both right and wrong at the same time.

Mons was sitting in the lobby reading the local paper. When the boys came down he looked at them conspiratorially, as if he had a secret.

"Do you guys know who's coming to town on Thursday?" he asked.

"No, Mr. Simonsen," Sigmund said. "We don't have the slightest idea."

"Diana Mortensen!"

The boys' surprise was intense and fake.

"No way!" Sigmund exclaimed.

"That's a bit of a surprise," Markus mumbled, blushing.

"Indeed," Mons said, satisfied. "A limousine is going to pick her up at the airport in Oslo. They're arranging a reception for her at the hotel, with dinner at Fishland. I guess this place is going to be crawling with press people."

"Yeah, you can definitely count on that," Sigmund said.

Mons winked at Markus.

"Listen, boys, I have an idea."

"We can't wait to hear it," Sigmund said.

"Well, as you know, I promised you two a dinner at Fishland. What if I tried to reserve a table for Thursday?"

"That's a brilliant idea," Sigmund said.

"Splendid," Markus mumbled.

Mons smiled at him.

"If you're lucky, maybe you'll get her autograph. That would really be something, wouldn't it?"

"Yeah," Markus said. "That would be something."

"I'll reserve the table right away," Mons said. "We'd better hope they're not full."

"Yes," Sigmund said, "we'd really better hope that."

"Because that would be a real shame," Markus said, crossing his fingers and hoping that the restaurant would be packed.

It wasn't. There was one table left, and they got it. Markus closed his eyes. If he could just quit thinking, everything would probably be fine. But to be able to quit thinking, he would have to stop thinking about how he had to stop thinking, and that was going to be hard to do when he finally met the woman he spent all of his time thinking about.

"What are you thinking about?" Mons asked.

"Nothing," Markus said.

"Why are you wearing a suit?"

"I don't know."

"Save it for Thursday," Mons said. "Tonight we're going out for pizza."

Markus spent the evening practicing not thinking about what he was thinking about. Both Mons and Sigmund were in very high spirits. They were gorging themselves on pepperoni pizza, and Markus tried to keep up as best he could.

The next morning Mons rented golfing equipment. He was

going to practice his putt on the rooftop putting green, while Markus and Sigmund checked out Horten. It didn't matter that it was still pouring down rain. A little rain is nothing to a real golfer, and Mons practiced his putting in a raincoat and the golf cap he'd borrowed from Sigmund while the boys splashed around in town and ate soft-serve ice cream and peanuts. Afterwards all three of them went to the naval museum, where they saw not only the statue of Captain Oscar Wisting, but also a number of other famous people including Captain Leif Welding Olsen, the first Norwegian killed during the German invasion on April 8, 1940. Sigmund was a fabulous guide. He knew most of what there was to know about the naval museum and made the visit into a real experience for the other two. Then there was dinner at the hotel and off to the movie theater, where they saw an American comedy that put both Mons and Sigmund in an even better mood than they had been in before. Markus's mood, on the other hand, was quickly sinking. There was only one night and then a morning left now. The countdown had begun, and it was impossible not to think. After he got into bed, he started counting the stripes on his pajama top. There were thirteen, exactly like he'd thought. He sighed, said good night to Sigmund, and turned off the light.

He sat up in bed with a start. He'd woken up with a feeling that something terrible was going to happen, but he had no idea where he was. He saw Sigmund standing over by the window, and all of a sudden he remembered everything. He quickly lay back down again, and wondered if he should try to sleep a little more. A half-hour delay before he got up, greeted the day and ...

"Look! It's not raining anymore!"

Sigmund pulled the curtains open and came over to the bed. Markus pretended he was sleeping.

"You have to wake up, Markus! Today's the day!"

Markus opened his eyes a crack. Yes, today was the day. And tomorrow it would be over. He always had thoughts like this when he had to go to the dentist, but this was much worse than having someone drill into your tooth. This was so awful that he couldn't even manage to look forward to the next day. Because after today, nothing would be the same. He was about to experience the biggest defeat of his life, and he was never going to be able to live it down. It would haunt him for as long as he lived. Because no matter how much he managed to convince himself that he was the son of a millionaire, the truth would eventually come out. He was convinced of that. And once it did, he would never be able to not think again. The memory of his awful meeting with Diana Mortensen would make him even more cowardly, even more embarrassed, and even more awkward than he already was. Then he really would be Wormster. For ever and ever. Slowly he got out of bed.

"Yeah," he said. "Today's the day."

CHAPTER 13 "What do you boys want?"

Mons looked up from the menu. He was sitting next to Sigmund facing out toward the restaurant. Markus was sitting on the other side of the table, staring at the wall behind them. He had plunked himself down there the instant they walked in. His dad had offered to switch places with him so he could have a good view of Diana Mortensen when she arrived, but he had refused. He wasn't actually that interested in movie stars, he'd said, and he would prefer to eat his dinner in peace and quiet. He had a faint hope that he could put off the meeting with Diana for a couple of days. When Mons asked wasn't he going to ask her for her autograph, he would say that he had quit collecting autographs. And when Sigmund winked at him, because he was sure Sigmund was going to, he would pretend he didn't notice. Maybe he'd even be so lucky as to come down with food poisoning so he could quietly disappear up to his room. There were lots of possibilities. He contemplated them all, but knew he couldn't rely on any of them.

"Fish," he said. "I think I'm going to have fish."

Mons laughed and responded, "Of course. I mean, after all, it is a fish restaurant. But what kind of fish would you like?"

"I think I'll have the wolffish with shrimp," Sigmund said, "and a soda, if that's all right."

"I'm going to have the flounder in a white wine sauce," Mons said. "Markus?"

"Do they have raw fish here?" Markus asked.

He had heard that it was possible for raw fish to spoil, although that was unlikely at such a fancy restaurant.

"They have gravlax," Mons said, somewhat astonished. "But why do you want to have raw fish?"

"I like raw fish."

"You've never told me that before."

"No, that's why I'm telling you now."

He had started sweating before they even got to the restaurant, and now his shirt was soaked through. He felt like a little fish himself. Sopping wet and on his way down to the bottom of the sea, where crabs and deadly predatory fish were waiting to devour him. His suit jacket was starting to get wet too, and his hands felt like sponges full of warm water. If he was forced to shake Diana Mortensen's hand over the course of the evening, they would both be drenched.

"And what would you like to drink, Markus?"

"Just water."

"Wouldn't you like a soda too?"

"Sure. Thanks."

"Of course you can just get water, if you'd rather have that."

"Yes, please."

"Which one do you want then, water or soda?"

"Perhaps he'd like both?" said the waiter, who was standing next to the table jotting down their order.

"Please. Thank you," Markus said.

The waiter left, and Mons started telling them fish stories from Lake Savalen, where he'd gone on vacation when he was a kid. Sigmund listened attentively. Markus didn't hear a word, but nodded mechanically every time his father paused.

"You know what I like to do? Fly-fish," Mons said. "That's pretty much the best way to do it, I think. I mean, I'm no expert; I can't even count the number of times my fly has gotten tangled up in a tree behind me. But it's definitely fun, that's for sure."

"Yeah, you're making me think it would be, Mr. Simonsen," Sigmund said.

"We should try to do it sometime, Markus," Mons said enthusiastically.

"What?"

"Fly-fish."

"Does it taste good?"

Mons was about to explain that "fly-fish" wasn't a kind of fish but rather a way of catching fish, but all of a sudden they heard laughter and loud voices from a group that had just walked into the restaurant. A man said:

"Yes, Diana, our fish is caught fresh daily, straight from the sea to your table."

Then a gleeful squeal was heard and a voice, which was impossible for anyone who'd seen *The Rich and the Powerful* not to recognize, cried out so loudly that everyone in the restaurant was forced to hear it:

"Oh, I love this country!"

Diana Mortensen had come home.

Sigmund and Mons sat there, each one holding a dinner roll

in his hand. They stared at Diana bug-eyed as they chewed automatically. They were looking right into a soap opera, from here in Horten, and Diana Mortensen was just as far away and just as close as Rebecca Jones had been when she stood on the ledge outside the window on the sixty-eighth floor. This wasn't real. This was an episode of the fanciful TV show about Diana Mortensen's life. And they were the audience. Markus stared at the wall. He felt as if he were on his way up to the top of the world's tallest roller coaster. He had a terrible sinking feeling in his stomach, but it was too late to call the whole thing off. Soon he would be plummeting downwards. That would be awful, but the worst part of all was the second when he reached the top. The instant the car stood almost completely still at the very top of the scaffolding. That's where he was now.

"Look, Markus," his dad whispered.

"She's right behind you," Sigmund whispered.

Their voices weren't voices. It was the wind up there whooshing past him.

"Turn around," Sigmund whispered. "Turn around, Markus!"

He didn't want to do it. But he had to. There was no getting out of it. He turned his head. Slowly and mechanically. Then he froze and sat motionless as the roller coaster barreled down.

Diana Mortensen was standing in the middle of the room. She was wearing a short, white skirt, a white silk blouse, and a white jacket. A gold chain with a shimmering green stone was hanging at her throat. Her hair was golden, her skin as pale as ivory, and the contours of her nipples were visible beneath her blouse. Her face was turned toward Markus. But he knew that she didn't see him. She was staring at three photographers, who were taking her picture as she smiled, showing her dazzlingly white teeth and enormous, astonishingly blue eyes. She tilted her head forward so that a strand of hair fell down, covering one of her eyes. She tossed her head back again, running her fingers through her hair, while sticking out her chest so that her nipples became even more obvious beneath her blouse. She threw up her arms and smiled at the other diners, as if to apologize for all the fuss. But the photographers didn't give up. They had her now, and they weren't going to let her go. The flashes flared at her as she smiled and smiled. Three bloodthirsty photographers had caught her in a trap. They were oblivious. They had no idea that the famous movie star Diana Mortensen was really a bird in a cage, who dreamed of spreading her wings and flying free, high in the sky where she could be herself and not the successful Barbie doll everyone thought she was.

Markus felt his cheeks starting to get hot. The heat spread through him. Behind his forehead. Like a fire in his brain. Invisible flames that consumed all the fear, shyness, and uncertainty he carried with him through his life. His thoughts burned until they weren't thoughts anymore, but a fiery hot rage that filled him and turned him into someone else. He wasn't Markus Simonsen anymore. He wasn't Markus Simonsen, Junior either. He was her brother. The only person in the world who understood how she was doing. He had also been small and scared once. But that was a long time ago. Now he was big brother, her bodyguard, Markus. The only one who could protect her from the wickedness of the world. He got up out of his chair.

"You can't ask her for her autograph now," his dad said. "You have to wait until they're done taking pictures."

Markus gave him an icy stare and said, "Sometimes a boy's got to do what a boy's got to do."

He turned away from the table and walked quickly past the photographers and over to Diana. She was still smiling when he reached her, but he saw that it was a forced smile. They were tormenting her, and it was his job to get rid of the tormentors.

"I'll help you, Diana," he said calmly. "I know how they can be."

Without waiting for a response, he turned toward the photographers.

"All right, people. I think that'll do it for today."

At first it was completely silent, then one of the photographers started to snicker. That was nothing new. People had laughed at him before. It didn't matter.

"Yes," he said calmly. "It's very funny, isn't it? Ha. Ha. I'm sure bothering people who can't defend themselves is one of the most amusing things you can think of. But now the party's over."

And the party was indeed over. It had gotten very quiet in the restaurant. Mons had gotten up from the table. His face was beet red. Sigmund tugged on his arm and whispered, "Sit down, Mr. Simonsen. I think it's best this way."

Mons sank down into his chair, his head sinking down between his shoulders.

"Don't you understand that she is a human being, a person." Markus said in a loud, clear voice. "A person! But you don't know what that is, do you? Because you think she's just a doll, don't you? A doll that you can do what you want to. You sneak around after her, everywhere, and you take these pictures just so you can earn enough money to be as rich as …" he couldn't think of anyone really rich "… as a king!"

At first it looked like the photographers were starting to get irritated, but suddenly the one who had laughed raised his camera and started taking pictures again. Markus flung out his arms to protect Diana, but the photographer just kept snapping away. And then the other two joined in. Their faces were hidden behind their cameras. They looked like monsters shooting out dangerous rays, but it wasn't Diana they were aiming at. It was him. Markus Simonsen, bodyguard.

"Go ahead and shoot!" he yelled. "We're not afraid of you!"

He heard footsteps behind him. It was Diana. She was at his side now. He put his arm around her protectively. She was still smiling. Yes, she looked almost cheerful. She put her arm around his waist. She seemed to feel more secure now. And she had every reason to. He wouldn't let her down.

"Yes, here we are!" he yelled. "You think you've got us trapped, but you haven't. Because we couldn't care less about you. We are just like birds. We want to fly … free and high. And you, you are just some miserable, wretched little … worms!"

He fell silent. Stood there without moving, without thinking. The flashes kept exploding, and Diana smiled. She patted him on the head and winked at the photographers.

"Oh, you're so sweet," she said. "What's your name?"

"I'm Markus," Markus said, "Markus Simonsen. That's my name."

That was a mistake. When he heard the sound of his own name, he wasn't able to avoid thinking anymore. The fire in his brain went out, and the thoughts raced through his head like a violent avalanche of snow and ice. What had he done? Why in the world was he standing here? At any rate, he had finally gone crazy now. Totally bonkers, completely crazy. He stared, blushing and helpless, past the photographers at Mons. He wasn't going to be much help. His dad was just as red and discombobulated as he was. Mr. Tomato, Junior and Mr. Tomato, Senior. He cringed and stared down at the floor.

The photographers had stopped taking pictures. Behind him he heard people mumbling something or other. A few people were laughing too. Both in front of him and behind him. He closed his eyes and wished he were invisible, but he wasn't. He was probably the most visible person in the restaurant. And tomorrow the most visible in the whole country, with his picture all over the news-papers and the whole kit and caboodle. A scandal at the age of thirteen. "Big Embarrassment for Small Fan at Fishland." "Crazed Boy Harasses Starlet, Likens to Bird."

He felt a hand on his shoulder. It was probably the police coming to remove him from the premises.

"I'm sorry," he muttered. "I didn't mean it."

He noticed that someone was leaning over him.

"Are you Markus?"

It wasn't the police.

"Markus Junior?"

The voice was low and soft and so close to his ear that the warm breath sent shivers down his spine. He nodded without making a sound and opened his eyes. Her face was so close to his. She kissed him on the cheek. He closed his eyes again and felt himself flying. Diana Mortensen took his hand and led him up into the heavens.

"So nice to meet you," she said loudly. "I've heard so much about you. We have so much to talk about."

She smiled radiantly. He tried to smile charmingly back. It was probably a little strained. Because he was on his way up into the heavens and really rather dizzy.

"I know how much a tennis ball weighs," he mumbled.

"I knew you had a sense of humor," Diana said and laughed.

As if on cue everyone started laughing. Aside from Mons, Sigmund, and him. But it wasn't a mean-spirited laughter; it was a pleasant, friendly, well-hello-there laughter. An oh-so-you-and-Diana-are-friends? laughter. In an instant he was the center of a flock of unknown, festive people, who were eager to meet the boy Diana had heard so much about. The photographers assured him that they did not want to pester Diana, but that they had been invited. Some of the guests smiled and said that it served the photographers right to be put in their places once in a while, but everyone agreed that he had picked a funny way to make his presence known and that he had almost fooled them all. Diana held his hand the whole time and smiled at him as if she were thrilled to see him. An elderly man who was clearly the host of her party asked if he'd like to sit with them, but Markus said he was here with his father. When he said that, Diana's eyes opened even wider than they were already.

"Your father's here?" she whispered.

He nodded.

"Yeah, he's sitting over there."

She stared past him, at the table where Mons was sitting, beet red, hunched over, and staring down at his plate. Sigmund was sitting next to him. He was looking at Diana, mesmerized, and when she looked over at them, he did something Markus had never seen him do before: He blushed.

"Do you think your father would like to come over to our table?" Diana asked.

Markus shook his head.

"No," he mumbled. "He's ... he's afraid of ... photographers."

Diana nodded.

"I understand. I bet that means he'd prefer if I didn't go over and say hello to him right now."

"No," Markus said quickly. "That's probably not a good idea."

Diana kept staring at Mons. He glanced up and met her gaze. She smiled discreetly. As quick as lightning he bent his head back down, picked up his knife and fork, and started scraping away at his plate, discovered that it was empty, set his utensils down, turned around, and looked out the window. Even the back of his neck was red.

"I can tell that he doesn't want to meet me right now," Diana whispered. "Could you tell him I said hello?"

Markus nodded.

"Where are you staying?"

"We're staying here at the hotel," Markus said. "Dad plays golf on the roof. I have to go now."

"I'm sure we'll see each other again," Diana said.

"Yes," Markus said, walking back over to his table just as the waiter brought their food.

"What in the world were you doing?" Mons whispered hoarsely.

"I was saying hello to Diana Mortensen," Markus said, taking a bite of his salmon. It actually tasted good.

"But … but … do you know her?"

"A little," Markus said. "I wrote and asked for her autograph. Then she answered, and after that we wrote a few letters to each other."

"You didn't tell me that," Mons said, lifting his glass.

"No," Sigmund said calmly. "I'd imagine there are a few things you don't know, Mr. Simonsen. It looks like she's raising her glass to toast you now."

Mons flinched as if he'd been stung by a wasp.

"What did you say?"

"She's raising her glass and she's looking at you. I think she wants to drink a toast with you … yup."

"Why in the world would she want to drink a toast with me?"

"Well, she probably thinks you look nice."

Mons glanced over at Diana. She smiled at him and he smiled stiffly back. She nodded and raised her glass.

"You have to raise your glass back, Mr. Simonsen," Sigmund said. "Otherwise it's impolite."

Mons raised his glass to Diana. He tried to do it in a way that could be interpreted both as if he were raising his glass to her and as if he just happened to be moving his arm that way. Diana interpreted it as a toast. Her smile widened. She took a little sip, and Mons couldn't believe his own eyes when she winked at him. He took a sip from his glass. It went down the wrong way and he coughed as noiselessly as he could. He made quite a bit of noise.

"I don't get it," he mumbled. "I absolutely don't get it. Did you write to her about me, Markus?"

"Just a little," Markus said, taking another bite of his salmon. It didn't taste quite as good now.

While they ate, Mons tried to find out what Markus and Diana had written to each other. Markus answered as evasively as he could, and Mons wasn't able to fully concentrate on the answers either. He kept looking over at Diana, and every time he did, their eyes would meet. By the time they were done eating, Markus wasn't the only one who was sweating. Mons needed to take a shower too. They paid and got up from the table. Diana did the same. *She must be going to the ladies' room.* When they walked into the lobby, she was standing there waiting for them. For a second Mons looked like he wanted to duck back into the restaurant again, but he changed his mind and kept moving straight ahead. She held her hand out to him.

"Thank you for coming," she said quietly.

Mechanically, he took her hand.

"So, I'm Markus's father," he said in a gravelly voice.

"Fancy finally getting to meet you," Diana said softly.

"Yeah, heh heh," Mons squeaked.

He let go of her hand and jogged over to the stairs, followed closely by his son.

Sigmund just stood there with Diana.

"He's kind of a quiet guy," he said by way of explanation.

It didn't seem like Diana had heard him. Her eyes were turned toward the empty stairs.

"I'm also kind of a quiet guy," Sigmund said.

Diana noticed him standing there.

"What did you say?"

"That, um, I … could I … maybe get … your autograph?"

CHAPTER 14 Mons accompanied the boys to their room. He was rather flustered and confused. So was Markus. Sigmund, on the other hand, was in complete control. He had Diana's autograph in his wallet and was very satisfied with his dinner. Mons had a strong sense that Sigmund was behind the whole thing; he just wasn't sure what the whole thing was.

"I demand an explanation!" Mons said angrily.

"And you'll get one, Mr. Simonsen," Sigmund said, "because I really think you're entitled to one."

"You do?" Mons said, a little calmer.

"Yes," Sigmund said. "Have a seat."

Markus was biting his lip and winking desperately at Sigmund. If he told Mons about Markus Senior and Markus Junior, the room was definitely going to explode.

"Are your eyes hurting you, Markus?" Mons asked.

"What? No. Um, I'm just …"

He looked at the clock.

"I'm just a little tired."

He held a hand in front of his mouth and pretended to yawn.

"It's about time we hit the sack. It's been a strenuous day. Aaaah, I'm beat. Good night, Dad."

It was useless. Mons sat down and Sigmund got a soda out of the minibar.

"Here you go, Mr. Simonsen. You probably need a little pick-me-up."

"I think I'll have a beer instead," Mons said.

"Well, anyway, I'm going to go to bed," Markus mumbled.

He started getting undressed, and while Sigmund started explaining he changed into his pajamas, climbed into bed, and pulled the comforter over his head. He pretended to fall asleep right away, but he heard every word they said.

Sigmund had many talents. Markus already knew from previous experience that he would probably make a brilliant astrophysicist or a talented advertising executive. Now he was demonstrating his diplomatic abilities. And they were nothing to sneeze at, either. A sense of uneasiness hung in the air as Mons sat down in the chair and opened his bottle of beer, but by the time Sigmund was done talking the atmosphere in the room was friendly and relaxed. Yes, almost cheerful. The ingenious peace negotiator had known exactly what to emphasize and what was better left unsaid.

He told Mons about how the court had treated Diana Mortensen unfairly when it ruled against her, denying her any compensation for the pictures of her exposed breast. He explained about the Help Diana Club, about the letters they'd written, how happy she was to get the letters, and how she'd really wanted to meet Markus while she was in Norway.

"Markus was the one who signed the letters," Sigmund said. "Personally, I don't like to draw attention to myself. Believe it or not, Mr. Simonsen, I prefer to stay out of the spotlight."

Mons had opened a second beer. He nodded.

"Me too," he said.

Vigorous snoring sounds could be heard from the bed.

"He's asleep," Sigmund said. "And, boy, has he earned it. You have a brave son, Mr. Simonsen."

Mons nodded.

"Yeah, he takes after his mother. Keep going, Sigmund."

Sigmund kept going. The time had come for confessions. He explained that they had actually known that Rebecca Jones was going to fall off the skyscraper, but that they had never intended for Mons to pay for the meal. The bet had just been a joke, or "a little prank" as Sigmund put it. He actually had brought money from home with clear instructions that he was to treat Mons and Markus to a good dinner. He took out his wallet and opened it.

"I wouldn't hear of it," Mons said in exasperation. "You're my guest."

Sigmund sighed.

"Well, good. Then that settles it. I'll assume there's no point in discussing it any further."

"None at all," Mons said satisfied. "Keep going! What did you write about me?"

The snoring from the bed got louder.

"Markus was the one who did the writing," Sigmund said.

"What did he write?"

It was dead silent under the comforter, but he need not have worried. The time had come for lies.

"He just told her how much he loves you."

"He did?"

The comforter moved up and down. Markus was breathing like a pair of bellows.

"Yeah, he wrote that you were the world's greatest dad. That you were honest, generous, and hated injustice."

"Did he really?"

Mons's voice was a little choked up.

"Yeah, but I have to admit one thing."

"What?"

"He also lied a little about you."

An energetic snore came from the bed.

"He lied?"

"Yeah. He wrote that you were the one who made us see how unfairly she'd been treated."

"He did? But why …?"

"I'm not sure, Mr. Simonsen, but I think it was because he's so incredibly modest. It was like he just couldn't bring himself to take the credit."

"I see," Mons said. His voice sounded quite choked up now, and he had tears in his eyes. "Markus always has been a modest kid. So that's why she was so happy to meet me."

"That's probably why."

"Markus deserves the credit; I don't want to take it away from him," Mons said. "We have to tell her the truth."

"You're so much like your son," Sigmund said, moved. "You're every bit as modest as he is."

"You think so?" Mons said.

"Yeah, I do."

"I'm going to go down and explain this to her right now."

"You don't have to do that, Mr. Simonsen. I'll do it."

"You will? Really?"

"I will," Sigmund said calmly. "It's the least I can do."

"Well, I think I'm going to go to bed then," Mons said, relieved.

"You do that. But please be careful when you close the door so you don't wake Markus up."

"I will. He's a great kid, isn't he, Sigmund?"

"The best, Mr. Simonsen. The very best!"

Mons tiptoed out of the room.

"You can come out now," Sigmund said. "The coast is clear."

Markus got out of bed and staggered into the middle of the room. He opened his mouth as if he wanted to say something. Then he changed his mind and got a bottle of soda out of the minibar. He drank a long swig, put the bottle down, and stared at Sigmund.

"You … you … How did you do that?"

"That's just the way I am," Sigmund said.

"What do we do now?"

"Now we go down and get Diana."

Markus dropped the bottle on the floor.

"But … but … You can't …"

"Relax," Sigmund said. "Listen to me."

Markus sat in front of the mirror in his hotel room and looked at his face. He smiled charmingly. There was Junior. Expert at social etiquette. He furrowed his brows. There was the bodyguard. Expert at getting rid of troublesome photographers. He sat completely still and just looked. There he was. Markus Simonsen. Thirteen years old. Expert at not being Markus Simonsen. He stared back at himself from inside the mirror. His face looked completely ordinary. Not happy, not sad, not even scared. Just slightly curious. Like someone who really wanted to get to know him. He nodded to the mirror. Smiled cautiously. Nodded again. His reflection opened its mouth, and he heard his voice whisper, "Don't leave me."

He lay down on the bed and stared up at the ceiling while he tried to think. Typical. Usually he struggled not to think but just this once, when he was actually trying to, he couldn't do it. He got up from the bed and started pacing back and forth. He had put on his tracksuit, like they'd agreed. He tried walking in different ways, but no matter what he did it felt just as awkward. How long had Sigmund been gone? Five minutes or half an hour? He had no clue. He stopped in front of the mirror, took out his comb, and started combing his hair. How many different hairdos were there in the world? A million? His reflection stared back at him unhappily. He looked himself in the eyes, and started thinking. Then he found the word he'd been looking for ever since Sigmund had left:

"No!"

"It took a little while, but here we are," Sigmund said as he opened the door and let Diana Mortensen into the room in front of him.

Markus didn't respond. He was sitting hunched over in front of the mirror in his normal clothes: pants that were slightly too big, a green shirt, and red socks. There was a piece of paper in front of him. Next to the piece of paper there was a ballpoint pen.

"You have a visitor," Sigmund said a little hesitantly.

This wasn't right. He had told Diana that Markus needed to talk to her about something important and, according to the plan, when they got there Markus was supposed to receive her in a casual and carefree manner, dressed in his tracksuit and with a glass of champagne from the minibar on a tray. He was supposed to tell her that, unfortunately, Markus Senior had been called home suddenly and unexpectedly. One of his mountain-climbing buddies was sick, and now he had to find someone to go in his place. They were leaving for Nepal in two days and, unfortunately, they probably wouldn't be back until November. Markus Junior and his good friend Sigmund would be staying in Norway. Junior was used to being alone, and Senior would be delighted if Diana might consider taking the boys along on a little sightseeing tour of Horten the next morning. This was the plan that Sigmund had come up with and that Markus had agreed to without protest. But now Markus had thought. He dropped his head down even further between his shoulders and kept staring at the piece of paper.

"Hi, Markus," Diana said. "What is it you wanted to tell me?"

He didn't respond.

"I think he's written a poem," Sigmund whispered. "He often does that when he's alone."

He hadn't given up yet and was holding out hope that Markus had just changed tactics.

"I do that too," Diana said. "I'm really fond of poetry."

"I didn't write a poem," Markus muttered.

"Are you working on your novel, then?" asked Sigmund, who was starting to get seriously nervous.

Markus stood up slowly. He was staring down at the floor and clutching the paper so hard in his hand that his knuckles turned white.

"It's a letter."

His voice was faint and hard to hear. He gulped and blushed. He was shy, scared, and completely himself.

"It's so nice to get letters," Diana said.

She said it in a friendly way, but slightly impatiently. After all, she was very fond of children, especially when there were photographers present. But when there weren't any photographers, she tired of them quickly.

"It's not to me," Markus said. "It's to you."

Diana lit up.

"Is it from your father?"

"No, it's from me."

Diana may not be the best actress in the world, but at least she managed to hide her disappointment and the enthusiasm in her voice sounded almost completely genuine.

"You wrote me a letter? How sweet of you, Markus."

She reached out her hand, but Markus said:

"I'd like to read it to you."

"I think I'll just duck out for a minute, actually," said Sigmund, who was already on his way out the door. It didn't work.

"Don't go," Markus said. "I want you to hear this too."

Sigmund turned around in the doorway.

"Would you like a glass of champagne, Ms. Mortensen?" he said.

Diana shook her head. She was looking at Markus, who was staring straight down at the floor just in front of her.

"Go ahead. Read," she said. "I don't bite."

"Heh heh," Sigmund chuckled tensely. He sat down on the bed, fearing the worst.

Markus read. Very slowly, very softly, and very clearly. He read to Diana and read to Sigmund, but most of all he read to himself:

> *Dear Diana Mortensen.*
>
> *I am Markus. Markus Simonsen. I am the one who wrote all the letters. They were all just lies. Dad isn't a millionaire, and therefore I am not the son of a millionaire either. Everyone calls me Wormster because I'm so scared all the time. I'm scared of everything a person can possibly be scared of. The only thing I'm good at is not being myself. That's very easy, but I don't know if everything is supposed to be so easy. I really want to try to do something hard too, and the hardest thing I know is being Markus. I'm sorry I lied to you, but I feel other things besides sorriness about it too. Because if I hadn't done that, I don't think I would have found out that I don't want to lie after all. Now I don't have anything else to write. Sorry.*
>
> *Greetings from Markus Simonsen. Age 13. Myself.*

He bowed stiffly to Diana and gave her the letter. After that he turned around, walked over to the window, and looked out.

Sigmund sat, fingering the comforter and pretending he wasn't there. Diana stood in the middle of the room with the letter in her hand.

Markus knew that anything could happen now. She might explode in rage, she might laugh at him, or she might just leave. It didn't matter. It was all over. Diana Mortensen. Markus Junior. It wasn't real. It was just a movie, all of it. But now the movie was over. He felt a kind of empty relief. It was real. He was standing here at the window and staring out at the stars. It was real. He heard her footsteps.

"Markus."

It was impossible to tell from her voice if she was mad or not. It didn't matter.

"There's Sirius," he said.

"What?"

Her voice was as soft as a puff of wind. Just a slight breeze before the storm breaks loose.

"Sirius eight years ago. That's how long it takes before the light gets to Earth. I wish I were there now."

"Where?"

Was her voice really that soft or was she just far away?

"On Sirius," he said. "Eight years ago."

She had put one hand on his shoulder. Now she gave it a squeeze. He turned his head and looked at her. Then the last thing he had ever expected happened. Diana Mortensen started to cry. Her body shook. She bit down on her lip while the tears rolled down her cheeks and painted stripes of black eye shadow across her pale face. She cried like a baby, in rapid little gasps, as she tried to dry away her tears with a small pink handkerchief that was quickly stained red, black, and whitish by all the colors from her face. She had let go of his shoulders and was holding her hands in front of her eyes as she bent her head down so that he could see that the hair by her scalp wasn't golden, but sand-colored. He wanted to stroke her hair, but didn't dare. He was only thirteen years old and had no idea how to comfort an unhappy movie star.

"I'm sorry," he mumbled.

She took her hands away from her eyes and raised her face toward him. Then she smiled. A sorrowful smile Markus had seen a hundred times before.

"How was that?" she said.

"How was what?"

"My tears. Did they seem real?"

"They were totally amazing," Sigmund confessed.

He had taken a seat on the bed and opened a bag of peanuts as he stared at Diana in admiration.

"I'm not such a bad crier, am I?" she said cheerfully. "I'm going to play Juliet in *Romeo and Juliet*. I have to practice all the time."

"Well, we won't get in your way," Sigmund said. "Will we, Markus?"

Markus didn't respond. Suddenly, in a flash, he understood everything. Not when she was crying, but when he saw the stripes on her cheeks, the sand-colored strands of hair by her scalp, and the smile that wasn't her own but some smile she'd learned in a movie studio far away. The Rebecca Jones smile. Then he had seen what she wasn't. The whitish skin wasn't hers. It was makeup. The golden hair wasn't hers. It was dyed. The red lips weren't hers. They were painted. Diana Mortensen wasn't Diana Mortensen.

"You don't have to lie," he said softly.

There was a "Hey!" from the bed.

"What did you say?" Diana asked.

Her eyes twinkled, but it didn't matter. He knew it wasn't genuine.

"I know how it is. I think it's extremely difficult to be me too," Markus said calmly.

Sigmund's bag of peanuts made a faint crinkling noise. Diana stared at Markus. He stared back. Underneath all the makeup on her face, a faint reddish color appeared. As if lipstick had been smeared across her cheeks. She opened her mouth. In complete seriousness, Markus said:

"You're blushing too."

Diana sat motionless. Her face got redder and redder, but she didn't say a word. The light from Sirius filtered in through the window.

"You wish you were there too, don't you?" Markus said.

Diana tried to smile again. She couldn't quite pull it off. Rebecca Jones was dead.

"But we're not seeing Sirius. We're seeing something that doesn't exist anymore."

Diana Mortensen said:

"My name's not even Diana. My name is Mette."

"Yeah," Markus said calmly. "I figured."

Sigmund had emptied the bag of peanuts and started on the potato chips. He was confused, self-effacing, and modest. The things that had transpired in this room over the last fifteen minutes had been too much even for his superior intellect, although the end result was what he'd expected. Diana, no, Mette Mortensen, and Markus

Junior, no, Markus Simonsen, had become the best of friends. Once she had finished crying, she had given Markus a hug and he had hugged back without blushing or anything, while Sigmund, who was used to being in control of the situation, just sat there feeling like an idiot. They had started laughing without Sigmund, for the life of him, being able to figure out what they were laughing at.

"Do they really call you Wormster?" she'd asked.

"Yeah," he'd replied and sighed deeply.

"Know what they used to call me?"

"Marilyn Monroe?" Sigmund volunteered without anyone noticing.

"They used to call me Meta-Mouse."

Then they laughed even more. Sigmund tried to laugh too, but it sounded kind of forced, so he helped himself to a potato chip instead while he waited for the next revelation. He didn't have to wait long.

"I'm actually a really bad actor," Mette Mortensen said.

"Me too," Markus said.

And then they laughed again. Sigmund didn't get why that was so funny, but he didn't say anything. He understood that there were times when even geniuses should keep quiet.

"That's why I got kicked off the show," Mette said. "The viewers thought I was mind-numbingly boring."

"The viewers are a bunch of idiots," Markus said.

"I've never met Robert De Niro."

"Me neither."

"I'm only on screen for eighteen seconds in *The Labyrinth of Love*."

"I'm not in it at all."

"That's Hollywood's loss," Mette Mortensen said.

"Yeah, right, I'm sure they're really bummed."

"My agent said the mouthwash ad was my last chance."

"How did it go?"

"It was awful. When it aired, mouthwash sales actually fell by twenty percent. They're hoping it'll go better in Norway. People here think I'm a star."

"You are a star," Markus said, and without knowing why, he added: "You're ... Sirius."

Sigmund felt like he *had* to say something.

"They're a bunch of jerks," he said.

They both looked at him.

"Who are?" Mette Mortensen said.

"Um ...," Sigmund said nervously. "You know, them."

He was searching desperately for the right words.

"I mean ... I mean ... that judge who wouldn't give you compensation for the pictures and stuff."

Mette laughed.

"But he was totally right to do that. My agent came up with that whole thing."

"Huh?"

"He thought it would be good for my career."

Now Sigmund had had enough. Without making a sound, he stood up and walked over to the door.

"I'm going to pop down to the lobby and, um ... play a little golf," he said.

When Sigmund left, Markus suddenly felt a little anxious, but when he looked at Mette he knew that she was just as nervous as he was.

"You won't tell anyone all this, will you?" she asked.

He shook his head.

"Not your friend either?"

"No. My word is his bond."

She laughed.

"It is not."

"Well, no, but he's really good at keeping secrets. When are you going back?"

"I'm not going back. When I go downstairs, I'm going to give an interview. I'm going to explain that I'm taking some time off because I'm tired of the whole jet-set life."

"Will they believe you?"

"They can believe whatever they want."

He thought for a minute.

"Di … Mette?"

"Yes."

"I was wondering if you could …"

"If I could what?"

"If you could ask those, um, photographers not to put the pictures of me in the paper."

"Why?"

"I don't know. It's so, um, embarrassing."

"I will," Mette said.

"What if they say no?"

"Then I'll refuse to give them the interview."

Markus breathed a sigh of relief.

"Thank you."

There was a brief silence. Neither of them knew quite what to say. They smiled at each other a little shyly.

"What are you going to do now?" Markus asked quietly.

"I'm going to work in my dad's store. Imagine that. Silly me in a store."

They both laughed.

"So what are you going to do, Markus?"

"I'm going to start middle school," said Markus, holding the door open for her.

CHAPTER 15 It was a Saturday in September, and it was starting to get dark earlier and earlier. The first month of middle school hadn't been quite as gruesome as he'd feared. There were still a few people who teased him, and he seemed to have brought the name Wormster with him from elementary school. But he was the one who had told everyone that that's what people usually called him:

"So, your name is Markus Simonsen," the teacher had said.

"Yes, but people usually call me Wormster."

The class had laughed, but the laughter was sort of more laid-back. It was kind of hard to tease him with it if he chose to use it himself.

"And I blush too," he'd said. "Pretty often, actually."

Then the laughter had gotten even more laid-back, and finally it died out almost completely.

He and Sigmund started out in the same homeroom, and they still took their long walks back and forth across the playground, engrossed in their peculiar conversations.

"Imagination," Markus would say, "isn't something you think. It's something you feel."

"You can't feel imagination, Markus …"

"Wormster."

"Right, Wormster. You have to think before you feel."

"No, you don't. You have to feel before you think."

"That's impossible. For example, you can't feel that the light from Sirius is over eight years old before you've thought it."

"You can't think about the light before you've felt it either."

They could keep going like this for ages, getting themselves all tangled up in discussions where they would never agree. No one understood why Markus and Sigmund were friends, but they didn't care.

"You don't have to understand everything all the time," Markus said, and for once Sigmund agreed.

Ellen Christine and Sigmund were dating, and Markus and Mona had kissed each other outside the snack bar one night in August. They had both blushed. It was really nice, but when she asked him if he could teach her the Markuska, he explained that he didn't actually know how to dance. He had only been pretending. Then she'd been really impressed and said that she wished more boys were as modest as he was. But none of them were. And Markus agreed. After all, nobody was him besides him.

This morning he was sitting in his room writing a letter to Robert De Niro. Which is to say that it wasn't actually him writing. It was the young Norwegian actress Marikken Simonsen. Writing in Norwegian! That way he didn't have to think about it. He would translate it later. Since he got a B– on his last English assignment, he figured it would go fine.

Marikken had noticed a hint of softness around Robert's lips and wondered if he were really as tough as he let on. Of course, it wasn't any of Marikken's business—she had just wanted to write and say that no matter how lonely he felt, there would always be an unemployed young actress in Norway who understood him. He didn't need to reply, but if it wasn't too much trouble, she would be thrilled if he could send his autograph to her little brother, Markus Simonsen. He was a good kid, but sadly not brave enough to write his own letter. In other words, he was unbelievably chicken. Yes, he might possibly be the world's biggest chicken. He was afraid of everything you could be afraid of in this world: heights, the dark, bicycles, glaciers, and girls.

As he wrote this, he felt more and more moved, and by the time he wrote, "But most of all he's afraid of being Markus," he was so deeply touched that a couple of tears dripped down onto the paper. He rubbed them into the paper so that the ink ran a little. That looked cool, but not cool enough. It was still like something was missing. He didn't know what.

"Is something wrong, Markus?"

Mons was standing in the doorway, looking at him with concern.

"Nope. Everything's fine, Dad."

"Are you crying?"

"No."

Mons looked as if he were about to say something stupid. Then he changed his mind and nodded.

"I understand," he said.

Markus smiled at him.

"Yeah, I know."

"A letter came for you."

"Oh?"

"Yeah … from Horten."

He handed the big gray envelope to Markus.

"Aren't you going to open it?"

"Dad, it's private."

"Oh, I guess it is," Mons said, walking slowly toward the door. He stood in the doorway and turned around to face Markus. He added, "I'll be in the living room if you need me."

Markus didn't respond, and Mons shut the door quietly behind him.

It wasn't a letter. It was a photograph.

Of Markus Simonsen, Junior, a.k.a. "the Bodyguard," with his arms outstretched. He had a stern look on his face. "Diana" Mortensen was standing behind him. She was smiling radiantly and staring at Markus, her eyes wide with surprise. At the bottom of the picture she'd written: TO MARKUS BEST WISHES FROM SIRIUS.

He put the picture on his desk and noted that he didn't feel sad. He was actually in a really good mood. He glanced down at his letter to Robert De Niro, grabbed the pen, and wrote "I'm Markus" at the bottom of the page.

Then he let out a sigh of satisfaction, folded up the letter, and went in to where his dad was sitting in the living room, pretending to read the paper.

"It's from Di … from Mette," Markus said, handing him the photograph.

"Yeah, I figured," Mons said. "How nice … But why does it say 'Best wishes from Sirius'?"

"Because it was such a long time ago," Markus Simonsen said, blushing.